HART to heart

M.E. CARTER

This is a work of fiction. Names, characters, places, brands, media, and incidents are either the product of the author's imagination or are used fictitiously. The author acknowledges the trademarked status and trademark owners of various products referenced in this work of fiction, which have been used without permission. The publication/use of these trademarks is not authorized, associated with, or sponsored by the trademark owners.

Copyright © 2015 by M.E. Carter

All rights reserved.
Without limiting the rights under copyright reserved above, no part of this publication may be reproduced, stored in or introduced into a retrieval system, or transmitted, in any form, or by any means (electronic, mechanical, photocopying, recording, or otherwise) without the prior written permission of the above copyright owner of this book.

First Edition: July 2015
Library of Congress Cataloging-in-Publication Data
Hart to Heart – 1st ed
ISBN-13: 978-1514768990
ISBN-10: 1514768992

To J, J, K, K,
and all the others we've lost.

When it seems the world has forgotten,
know that we will NEVER forget you.

AUTHOR'S NOTE

When I wrote my debut novel, *Change of Hart*, it was supposed to be a standalone novel. Technically it still is. But a strange thing happened . . . as I got down to the last few chapters in CoH, this continuation started rolling around in my brain. I'm not quite sure why the characters told me this additional story, but they did.

I feel strongly that once you find the love of your life and get married, happily ever after doesn't just happen. Life happens. Terrible shit happens. And the Harts are about to go through some of the worst things any married couple can experience. So be forewarned.

There are some of you out there who will read this with an overly critical eye, and that's fine. But please be aware that a *lot* of research has gone into this book. I have consulted with an entire team of people directly involved in these issues to make sure I got it right. I made sure that things that were true five years ago about these topics but are no longer the case today were written accordingly. Were there a few liberties taken for literary purposes? Sure. But the overall, vast majority of the technical details have been verified by multiple sources.

As I say that, please don't let the technical parts take away from the overall story. It's an important one that I feel needs to be told because it's part of my heart.

So with all that being said, I now give you *Hart to Heart*.

Chapter ONE

"You know I'm taking credit for this whole thing, right?" Lindsay asked as she took a drink out of her big-ass wine glass. No telling how many glasses she'd had already.

"How the hell do you come to that conclusion?" I asked with a laugh as I finally tore my gaze away from my beautiful bride to look at Lindsay. "I *paid* for this wedding. Hell, I paid for you to get here!"

She waved me off with a flick of her hand while I looked around the patio. The air in Scotland was crisp at night, even in the middle of June. But that didn't stop the party. I caught another glimpse of Addison dancing with Jaxon. I've never seen that beautiful smile of hers look brighter. She was having the time of her life, and who could blame her? We were surrounded by our closest friends and family, who just cheered us on as we became man and wife.

Wow, I thought to myself. *She's my wife*. That was going to sound surreal for a while.

"Sure, you paid for the *wedding,*" Lindsay remarked. "But if I hadn't asked you to come speak at the school, you would have never met Jaxon. And if you'd never met Jaxon, you would have never met Addison. See? I'm taking credit."

I laughed as she took another swig. "Ya know," I started, leaning my elbows on the high round table we were standing at, "I'm the one who found you online. I'm the one who friended you. So technically, it all started with me reaching out to you."

Lindsay waved me off again as Deuce came bounding up, drunk as all get out.

"Dude," he said, practically falling into me. "Someone is finally getting laid tonight! I bet you can't wait to get your woman back to your room and uh, uh, uh," he said while pumping his hips and making a fool out of himself.

I just shook my head and tried to ignore him, but leave it to Lindsay to egg him on.

"Wait, wait, wait," she said, leaning in closer. "What do you mean he's *finally* getting laid, Deuce? What am I missing?"

Deuce threw his head back and laughed like it was the funniest thing he'd ever heard. "You didn't know this?" Lindsay shook her head while I slid my hand down my face. I really needed to find a new best friend. "Mr. Hart, Mr. Studmuffin himself, got cut off before the wedding!"

I groaned. "Don't you have a wife and son you should be hanging out with right now?" I asked.

He slapped me on the back and squeezed my shoulder. "They're too busy on the dance floor," he answered, gesturing a few feet away where Vanessa was spinning baby Trace around in time to the music. Trace was his nickname, since his given name was Michael Johnson the Third. As in uno, dos . . .

Trace. Yeah, it wasn't spelled like the number, but when they came up with the idea, they were pretty adamant that they didn't want the baby to have to explain the spelling of his name for the rest of his life.

"Tonight will be the first time he's gotten laid in six weeks!" Deuce continued while he and Lindsay both laughed at my sexual frustration. Don't get me wrong, it sucked that I hadn't been with Addison in that long, but she wanted our first time as husband and wife to be like the first time all over again. Of course, that meant I was going to have to control myself tonight so I could last more than ten seconds. But I understood where she was coming from, and frankly, I'd do anything to make her happy. So that's just what I did.

"What's so funny?" Elaine asked as she approached the table. Sara was still on the dance floor with all the bridesmaids living it up.

"Nothing much," I said sarcastically. "They're just laughing at my sex life."

"Nah," Deuce said with a serious look on his face. "We're laughing at your lack of one." He and Lindsay burst out laughing again. They really needed to be cut off at the bar.

Elaine gave Deuce a blank look and turned back to me. "Well," she said, "I'm not sure I want to know what that's about. But it's gotta be safer over here than on the dance floor right now."

We looked over to see all the single ladies in a small crowd, ready to catch the bouquet Addison was about to toss over her shoulder. And by all the single ladies, I meant all of Addison's school-aged nieces; Sara, Elaine's girlfriend; and Samantha, Addison's sister-in-law. Part of me wanted to go protect those little girls from what was sure to be a rougher play than I had ever been involved with on the field. The other part of me was almost giddy with excitement to see how this was gonna go down. Sara and Samantha were both ruthlessly competitive when it came to something they wanted, and I knew both of them were chomping at the bit to finally settle down. So who would claim the honor of being the next hypothetical bride to be? The anticipation made the topic of my sex life old news quickly.

"One . . . two . . . three . . ." Addison yelled before throwing the flowers over her shoulder. It couldn't have been better if it were in slow motion. The bouquet sailed in a perfect arch, and right as it dropped into Samantha's arms, Sara shoved her out of the way and caught it. I couldn't help but laugh at the scowl on Samantha's face when she realized what had happened.

"Shit," Elaine groaned, dropping her head on the table. "I do *not* want to start planning a wedding."

The rest of us were still belly laughing as Sara bounded over excitedly.

"Did you see?" she exclaimed, Elaine's head popping up off the table with a forced smile on her face as she turned to look at Sara. "Did you see me catch it?"

"I didn't just see you catch it," Deuce said. "I saw you shut Samantha down!" He raised his hand over the table as Sara slapped him a high five with a big grin on her face.

"Nice job, babe," Elaine said, putting her arm around Sara's waist and then taking a nice long swig of her Scottish beer.

"I think that means you're up, Hart," Lindsay said, pointing to the dance floor. Addison was looking at me. When she saw me look back at her, she crooked her finger at me, beckoning me to join her.

"Looks like I'm needed," I said, downing the last of my

drink. "Enjoy making your wedding plans, Elaine."

I heard her groan again as I walked towards my wife. I'm pretty sure my smile was just as big as hers at that moment. Once I got to her, I grabbed her hand and spun her around.

"Finally remembered you have a husband that you've been ditching all night to dance with your friends?" I joked. She just kept grinning.

"I've been right here the whole time, lover boy," she chided. "You could have danced with me anytime."

"I was having too much fun just watching you," I said honestly. "But I'm ready to dance with you now."

"No can do," she said with a glint in her eye. "I've thrown the bouquet. Now it's time for you to find my garter."

"While I'm not opposed to sticking my hand up your dress," I said, wiggling my eyebrows, "you do realize, with the exception of our son and Tracy's son, there's only like one single man here."

"Just go with it, Jason," she said huskily. Then she gave me a slow, sensual kiss. When I finally broke away from her and looked up, someone had put a chair on the dance floor and started some old-timey stripper-sounding music.

"I guess that's my cue," I said, guiding her to the chair and sitting her down. I walked around her a few times, like I was trying to figure out this puzzle. But I knew what I was going to do. I had already thought the entire scenario through. I knelt down in front of her, grabbed her feet, and slid my hands up her legs. Then I flung the poufy skirt of her dress over my head until I was all the way underneath.

I could hear the laughter and the whistles and Deuce yelling, "Get 'er done!" I couldn't help chuckling under my breath at that. But I was on a mission to find a garter, and while I knew the general vicinity, I was gonna take my sweet time finding it.

"Jason," Addison said as I started kissing the inside of her knee. "Ohmygod, stop!" she giggled. "Just get the garter and get out!"

I ignored her as I kissed up one thigh as high as I could without people seeing my head bob between her legs, and down the other until my lips brushed across the garter. I grabbed it with my teeth and slid it all the way down her leg and over her foot. It was no easy feat to do that with only my teeth. I almost got stuck on the heel of her shoe.

Once I got out from under her skirt, being careful that I didn't accidentally make her flash the guests, I stood up and took a bow amid the round of applause that was, no doubt, being led by Deuce.

"You're insane," Addison said with a smile as I leaned down to kiss her.

"Only for you, babe," I said, dropping my lips to hers. Then I walked straight over to Adam, who was paying more attention to flirting with Samantha than he was to the show on the dance floor.

"I believe this belongs to you," I said as I put the garter around his head like a headband.

"Really?" he asked. "There aren't any other single guys you can put a garter on? That's been around your wife's thigh all day, douchebag."

"Sorry, my man," I said, slapping him on the back. "You, Jaxon, and Ryder are it."

"Who the hell is Ryder?" he asked, snatching the garter off his head and dropping it on the table in front of him.

I rolled my eyes. "Tracy's son." He looked at me with a blank stare. "Addison's nephew," I continued. He just shrugged as if none of it rang a bell.

"Nice, dude. You've only spent the last week with this family. Anyway, since the two boys are over there hunting for fireflies with Emma, and are, ya know, *children*"—I gestured my head toward the grassy area just off the patio, where the kids were playing—"I think they're too busy to worry about who gets the garter. So it defaults to you."

I heard him grumble as I headed back to the dance floor.

"I was wondering if you were coming back," Addison said as I pulled her to me and started slow dancing with her.

"Just had to make sure Samantha knew all hope wasn't lost," I said with a smirk.

Addison giggled. "That's it. Encourage her man-hunt. I'm sure Adam will thank you in a month when he can't get rid of her."

"Hey, if he's dumb enough to fall into that trap, there's nothing I can do to stop him at this point."

Addison laid her head on my chest, and I tucked my head down to her neck, breathing her in and just enjoying the peacefulness of the moment. We really had made the right decision going to Scotland for our wedding.

Addison had finally gotten used to the notoriety that surrounded me. We'd been together for close to two years, so she kind of had to. But she still didn't care for it. It was important to her that any pictures of us on our wedding day were taken on our terms and not as some shady attempt to sell a magazine. Not only did Scotland provide the most beautiful landscape I had ever seen, but no one knew, nor cared, who we were, which made moments like these damn near perfect.

"So I have this fantasy," Addison said quietly. My head jerked back to look down at her as those five little words caught all my attention. I hadn't had sex in six weeks. I was more than intrigued now.

"Um . . . wha . . . what exactly is happening in this fantasy?" I stuttered, my eyebrows raised in question.

She smirked up at me and pretended to be shy about what she was about to say. But I knew better. She had me by the balls, and she knew it. I could feel myself getting riled up already, and nothing was even going on.

"I was thinking about you and me," she said, smoothing out the fabric of my tux vest absentmindedly. "Having sex."

"Uh huh," I said, completely engrossed in what she was saying.

"While you're naked." She looked up at me with her bright eyes. "And I'm in my wedding dress."

"Done. Let's go," I said, grabbing her hand and dragging her off the dance floor, toward the castle we were all staying in.

"Jason!" she laughed. "We can't go yet! We're in the middle of our wedding reception."

I turned around at her protest and moped as I walked back toward her. "I have been with these people all week long. I haven't been with just you in six weeks. You know all those things you needed for the wedding? Something old, something new, something borrowed?" She nodded. "I brought the blue. It's in my pants right now. Can't we please go?"

"Tell ya what," she said, putting her arms around my waist and pulling me close. "How about we take the next half hour to make the rounds and say our goodbyes. And then we'll head back to our wing."

I took a deep breath and sighed. "Fine. I've waited this long. What's another thirty minutes?" I whined.

She smiled and took my hand to guide me around the patio area to chat with everyone one last time, making sure my mom knew she was taking over Jaxon duty for the remainder of the night. It took longer than thirty minutes by the time we got to Deuce and Vanessa. He seemed to know exactly why we were saying goodbye and was determined to prolong my torture as long as possible. But finally, *finally*, she and I were alone and headed to our private wing of the castle.

We walked hand in hand down the long corridor on our way to the room. We were staying in Balfour Castle on the Island of Shapinsay. It was massive and completely secluded. As castles in Scotland go, Balfour was one of the younger ones, having been built in the late eighteenth century. It had apparently fallen apart after World War II but was renovated after that, and you would never be able to tell there was ever anything wrong. Now, of course, it had all the modern amenities we could ever need to feel like we were on vacation, without taking away the castle feel. It cost a lot to rent it for the week, but there was a whole lot to do on that tiny little island. And it was worth it to fit all our friends and family with room to spare *and* have an additional wing for Addison and me to be alone.

I couldn't help but feel a little nervous as I opened the door to our suite. I knew how important this night was for Addison, and I didn't want to blow it. At the same time, I was so ready I could've exploded right then and there.

Addison walked through the door, and I heard her gasp.

"Jason, it's breathtaking in here!"

I'd been staying in here since we'd arrived, but she hadn't seen it yet. The room was about the size of the entire downstairs in her little house back in Flower Mound, Texas. While it had beautiful, ornate furniture scattered around the room, the two most impressive parts were the view and the bed.

Addison immediately went to the glass doors and slid them open, stepping out to the balcony. We could still hear our family partying the night away with no sounds of stopping anytime soon. That was fine by me. I planned to be busy for a while.

I came up behind Addison and put my arms around her waist, kissing her gently in the crook of her neck.

"Thank you for the most wonderful day of my life," Addison said quietly. "It was perfect."

"You're perfect," I replied. "And you're mine now. You have no idea how that makes me feel."

"Tell me," she said as she tilted her head to give me better access to her neck.

I continued to kiss a line up to her jaw while thinking carefully through my words. I wasn't sure I could even articulate how happy this day had made me, but I was damn sure gonna try.

"It makes me feel like my life finally has meaning," I said. "Football used to be my life, but I always knew it was only temporary. Once it was over, I'd have to find myself all over again. But I feel like you've given me the most important part of who I am. Everything else is what I do. But you and our family, it's who I am. I am so grateful that you decided it was worth taking a chance on me. Because you're the other half of me that was missing. I just didn't know it until I found you," I said before continuing my venture on her neck.

"Jason?"

"Hmm?" I said lazily.

"Let's get you naked."

My head snapped up, and it took me about half a beat to pull her back into the room and close the sliding glass doors.

"You afraid they're gonna hear you if we leave the doors open?" Addison chided playfully.

"No," I argued. "I'm afraid they're gonna hear *you* when

you scream my name here in about five minutes."

She smirked. "Five minutes, huh?"

"Yep," I said with a smile. "And in seven minutes. And in ten minutes. Again in about fifteen minutes. And maybe again at the twenty-minute mark."

Addison blushed, and I watched as her breathing picked up in anticipation.

"Well then," she said. "I guess you'd better get naked and on that bed so I can live out my fantasy."

I smiled as I did a slow striptease for her. She just leaned back against the bed and watched, taking in every part of me as it became visible to her. I watched her face when I finally stripped off my boxer briefs and sprang free. When she licked her lips, I knew the past six weeks had been just as hard on her as they were on me.

As I ripped the comforter off the bed and lay down in the middle of the sheets, I watched her hike up her skirt and pull her white lace panties off. She tossed them at my head, and I grabbed them, quickly bringing them to my nose to inhale her scent.

"That's so gross," she said with a giggle. "You know that right?"

"Don't care," I said huskily. "Baby, you'd better get up here. I don't want to ruin your fantasy, but now that I've smelled you again, I'm losing my self-control quickly."

She smiled and crawled onto the bed, over me and into my arms, kissing me with all the passion she'd built up over the weeks. Once she got her fill of my lips and tongue, she shifted back and onto her knees, hiking up her dress and positioning herself above me.

She slid down until I was buried between her hips. My eyes closed and head rolled back at the feel of her after so long. She was right. It felt like the first time all over again. She was hot and wet and tight and *mine*. I went to grab her hips when I heard her giggle, and I suddenly noticed I was being smothered.

"What the fuck is this?" I asked as I started digging my way free, sex temporarily forgotten. A couple of seconds later, I could see Addison's face as she laughed.

"I guess I didn't take into account how big my skirt is," she said, still laughing.

"This is not nearly as sexy when I get buried underneath all the petticoat shit." I laughed, causing her to gasp.

"What?" I asked.

"Oh, that felt good when you laughed," she said, dropping her head back with a heavy breath. I groaned when her hips moved and she started riding me. I moved my hands back under her skirt and grabbed her hips, grinding her closer to me. Within minutes, I was being smothered again, but I didn't care.

I could hear Addison's breathing get ragged as she continued to ride me, chasing her orgasm. I could tell she was getting close, so I brushed her clit with my thumb, sending her over the edge.

"Ohmygod, Jason!" she cried out as she spasmed around me. Moments later, I moaned my own release, which seemed to go on and on and on.

We took a few minutes to catch our breath before digging me out of the petticoat thing again. When I finally felt the rush of cool air across my face, I put my hands behind my head and smiled up at my wife.

"Was that everything your fantasy made it out to be?" I asked her with a grin.

"Well, I wasn't expecting to not be able to see you, that's for sure," she answered. "But after six weeks, I'm not sure how much I was noticing anyway."

I laughed. "I'll admit, there is something to be said for letting it all build up for that long."

"I think the novelty of this dress has worn off now," she said, rising to her knees. We both winced as I slid out of her. "Would you help me out of it before we start getting all these pins out of my hair?"

We never got to the pins that night. As soon as the dress came off, I was ready to go for round two. It was just as good as the first time. Only this time, we stared into each other's eyes the whole time.

Chapter TWO

I was sitting outside late the next morning with Jaxon asleep on my lap when Deuce finally stumbled out the doors with sunglasses on and dropped into the seat across the table from me. The clean-up crew was busy stacking chairs and moving centerpieces from tables. Everyone else was inside, probably packing for their flight home. Addison and I would be staying in Scotland for another week for our honeymoon.

"Want a goat cheese omelet?" I asked Deuce, already knowing the answer.

He grimaced and held up his hand in protest as he grabbed the pitcher in front of him. "Nothing for me except orange juice," he said, pouring himself a glass.

"Long night?" I chided.

"You are an asshole for having an open bar," he said, sipping on his orange juice. "I'm still trying to decide if it was worth it."

"Let me know once you get to thirty-thousand feet," I said with a smile.

"Ugh," he responded, looking like he might upchuck at any moment. "I'm so glad Vanessa and I are only going to London. I don't think I could take a twelve-hour flight today."

"Serves you right for being such a douchebag last night," I said, shifting my legs and trying not to drop Jaxon in the process.

He chuckled. "I'm assuming you're going to be a lot harder to piss off now that you're more relaxed?"

"I don't know about that," I answered. "You seem to do a pretty good job pissing me off by just being you."

Deuce took a longer sip of his juice and grabbed a pastry off the table, taking a small bite, testing out his gag reflex. "What's going on here?" he asked, gesturing towards Jaxon, who was still asleep.

"I'm not sure," I said, looking down and smoothing his hair back off his face. "He said he wasn't feeling good. Addison gave him some Tylenol 'cause he had a little fever, and he's been knocked out ever since." I looked back up at Deuce. "You may want to keep an eye on Trace for a couple days since they've been playing together so much."

"I'm sure Vanessa's already rubbing some oils all over him and doing a chant or some shit like that," he said dismissively, taking another bite of the pastry. "She has oils for *everything*. Got a cold? Rub some oil on your chest. Sore throat? Put an oil under your tongue. Need to take a shit? Rub this oil on your ass," he said, shaking his head. "I swear it's like we live in a jungle with all the different smells in our house."

I chuckled. "I wouldn't let Vanessa hear you say that. She takes that shit seriously."

"And that's fine," Deuce said with his hands up in a defensive pose. "I'm sure there are some nice hocus pocus benefits to it. But if I need to take a shit, I'd rather drink some MiraLAX and sit on the pot for a while with a crossword puzzle."

Deuce was pouring himself another glass of orange juice when Adam joined us. He was acting really weird, not making eye contact. Being very quiet. Obviously avoiding telling us about his night. I just stared at him until he finally looked up at me.

"What?" he asked as he reached over to put some fruit on a plate.

"You know what," I answered, still not taking my eyes off him.

"Yeah," Deuce added. "Did you hit it last night?"

Adam scrunched his nose and paused what he was doing. I just started laughing.

"You did, didn't you!" I accused, still laughing. When Adam didn't answer, I kept going. "Seriously? Samantha? You realize what kind of trouble you're in now, right?"

"Aww, shit," Deuce said, sitting back in his chair. "I hope you weren't planning on staying single, because you are not getting rid of her anytime soon."

Adam groaned and put his face in his hands. "I don't know what happened. We were just talking, and she started getting flirty, and . . ."

"Shoving her tits in your face and squeezing your ass," Deuce finished for him. "We've all been there, man."

"That's not what happened," Adam defended.

I looked at him and laughed again. "Don't deny it. Deuce is right . . . we've *all* been there, Adam. I'm sure that's exactly what happened."

"Fine." He sighed. "But what do I do now? She's a nice girl . . ."

Deuce and I interrupted him with our laughs.

"Shut up, you guys," Adam said. "I'll figure out something. Maybe it's just a romantic Scotland thing or something."

"Sure," I said sarcastically, watching Deuce try to control his laughter. "I'm sure that's what it was."

"Anyway," Adam said, picking up his plate again and filling it up with more food, "I wanted to talk to you, Jason."

"What about?" I asked, shifting Jaxon when he started drooping off my lap again.

"We need to talk about what kind of non-profit you want to start up," he said as I groaned.

Ever since Adam had become my manager, he'd been bugging me to start a non-profit organization. Something about boosting my public image or some shit. As a side bonus, it could be used as a tax write-off since my money would be donated to the organization to make it stay afloat. It was a good idea. The problem was, there weren't any particular causes I was all that passionate about.

"Do we really have to talk about that now, man?" I asked. "I got married yesterday. I'm starting my honeymoon without you losers today."

"And he finally got laid last night," Deuce added. "Give him a minute to start thinking with the right head again."

I just ignored the interruption. "Look," I said. "When Addison and I get back, I'll really start to think about it. Maybe she has some better ideas than I do."

"I can work with that," Adam said as he bit into a strawberry. Just then, the doors opened again. Samantha walked out and Adam started choking on his strawberry. Deuce was still pounding him on the back when my mother came out a few seconds later.

"How's he doing," she asked me, kissing me on the head

and patting my shoulder before sitting down right next to me.

"He ate a little bit of fruit and then climbed up on my lap and fell asleep. He's been out for about thirty minutes. I hope he's well enough to fly home today."

"I'm sure he'll be fine," my mother said. "Kids get fevers all the time for the littlest thing. It was a big day for him yesterday. His body is probably just worn out."

We sat there for a couple more hours, enjoying the view and each other's company before everyone headed to the airport to fly home.

Chapter THREE

I woke up with sunlight in my eyes. Apparently we had fallen asleep with the blinds open, which explained why I was awake so early.

Addison and I had stayed in Scotland for an extra week, touring the countryside and exploring the city of Edinburgh. It had been a fantastic trip. But five days after getting back, jet lag was still killing us.

As I stretched my arms and legs and yawned, I looked over at Addison and felt myself get hard again. There was something about waking up next to my *wife* that made me horny just about all the time. So I rolled over and wrapped myself around her, kissing her neck and bare shoulder.

Apparently we had fallen asleep without clothes again, too. Not that I was complaining.

I felt her wake up and moan my name, encouraging me to devour the rest of her. "That feels so good," she said sleepily, reaching up to cup my cheek. I continued kissing down her arm until I reached her hand and rolled her onto her back, pinning her hand above her head as I settled on top of her.

"Good morning," I said as I kissed down the front of her chest. "Sleep well?"

"I was," she said. "But waking up is much better."

"Good," I said, making my way up to her mouth, morning breath be damned. "Today's gonna be a big day. I think we need to work out some of our anxiety."

"Oh you do, do you?" she asked with a smile as she brought her other hand up to join the first above her head. "I think that sounds like a fabulous idea."

I pulled the sheets over us and positioned myself between her legs. Just as I began to push inside her, the door flew open and Jaxon came barreling in.

"Get up, get up, get up! Today's the day! Get up!" he screamed as he ran around the room. When he saw us on the bed, he stopped dead in his tracks and looked back and forth between Addison and me several times. "What are you doing?" he asked.

"Wrestling," I answered without missing a beat.

"How come?"

"'Cause your mom woke me up, so I was getting ready to tickle her."

He paused in thought for a second. "Well do that later! Get up, today's the day!" he yelled and ran back out of the room.

I looked down at Addison, who had a shocked expression on her face. Then she started laughing.

"Ohmygod, how did you think of that so fast?"

"I walked in on my mom and dad once when I was a kid," I explained. "That's exactly what my dad said to me."

Addison moved her hands out from under mine and grabbed my face, pulling me in for a kiss. "Well done. First day on the job and you're already blowing this daddy thing out of the water."

"Don't compliment me yet," I said as I got up and shut the door Jax had left wide open. "That's still your son we're talking about."

"Don't get used to saying that, or I'll turn it around on you one of these days," she said as she walked towards the bathroom. I followed her into the shower, staring at her ass the whole way.

After a quick yet dirty shower, I dressed in some khakis and a blue polo and met Jax in the kitchen to make sure he was dressed.

I whistled when I saw him. "You look nice, Jax." He had chosen to wear some black slacks and a green button-down shirt. He was even wearing the black dress shoes from the wedding that he hated so much. I was genuinely impressed.

"Yeah, well I don't want the judge to think you guys make me wear dirty clothes or something. Then she might not let you adopt me."

I ruffled his hair as I walked by to get the coffee maker started. "That's not gonna happen, buddy. We've already done everything we needed to do. Today just makes it official."

And it was true. Per the State of Texas, a child couldn't be adopted until he had lived with the adoptive parent for six months. So just four days after Christmas, Addison, Jaxon and I had moved into a four-thousand-square-foot home in a gated community around the corner from their old house. Within a week of moving in, I had filled out all the paperwork to get all my background checks done and had set an appointment to have someone come out and do an official home study. The questions they asked during the home study were extremely personal, some almost offensive. But if that's what it took to convince the state that I could be a good father to Jaxon, then I was willing.

Now here we were, on June twenty-ninth, exactly six months from the date we moved in, getting ready to make Jaxon mine forever. I had to admit, I was probably more excited than he was. But I was still trying to be a good parent, so I couldn't let some things slide.

"Jax," I said as the coffee percolated. "What's the rule about you barging into our room?"

"I'm supposed to knock first."

"And how come?"

"Because you need your privacy."

"Exactly."

"But you were just wrestling," he argued.

"I know that, Jaxon," I responded, trying not to grin. "But what if your mom had been getting in the shower or something?"

He grimaced. "Like if she was naked?"

"Yeah. You're nine years old. You're too old to see your mom naked."

"You're thirty-one. How come you do?"

I opened my mouth and shut it again. I wasn't exactly sure how to answer this one.

"How come you do what?" Addison asked as she walked into the kitchen in her bathrobe, kissing Jax on the head and heading for the coffee pot.

"How come Jason can be in the room when you're naked?" he asked her.

Her eyebrows shot up and she looked over at me.

"He stumped me," I whispered. "I don't know the right answer."

Addison chuckled and grabbed two mugs from the cabinet and handed me one. The coffee pot wasn't full yet, but she wasn't one to patiently wait for coffee.

"Because we're married, Jaxon," she said nonchalantly as she filled her mug, leaving just enough room for some milk and sugar. "Someday, when you're married, you can be in the room when your wife is naked, too."

"Ew," he said, grimacing again. "That's gross. I'd rather eat a bug." Then he hopped off the stool and headed to the family room, probably to play some video games while we got ready to leave.

"There's never a right answer," Addison said as she walked around me, her coffee mug in hand as she headed back to the bedroom. "There's just the simplest answer that you can come up with. If it doesn't work, you can always fall back on the old, 'Because I said so.'" She flashed a quick smile at me over her shoulder before disappearing down the hall.

Thirty minutes later, Jax had whooped me in Minecraft—which I couldn't figure out since it just looked like we were playing Legos on TV—when Addison was finally ready to go get pancakes. It had become our little tradition. Every time there was a special occasion, whether it be the first day of school, straight A's on a report card, or the end of the football season, we went out for pancakes. With it being Adoption Day, it just seemed right.

After stuffing ourselves, we jumped back in my truck and headed to Downtown Dallas to the courthouse. I wasn't quite sure how many cases were on the docket, or even how many of those were adoptions. But I didn't care. I'd wait all day if I had to.

Once we finally made it through security, gave a few autographs and took a few pictures, we finally made it up to Courtroom Seven. My mom, Rick, Mick, and Adam were all waiting for us there.

"Are you ready to officially be a dad?" my mom asked as she hugged me tight.

"I don't know," I answered. "It depends on if you're ready to be a grandma."

"You know I love that little boy with all my heart," she said, glancing at Jaxon adoringly as he told Adam all about how he destroyed my building with a creeper or something this morning.

"Me too, Ma," I agreed before turning to Mick. "How are you feeling about all this today, Mick?" I asked, shaking his hand and patting him on the shoulder.

"Well," he said, "I'm not gonna say it's not bittersweet. But I've really been thinking about it, and frankly, I think Austin would give his blessing right now if he could. You've been a wonderful role model to Jax. I don't think either one of us could have picked a better man to be in his life."

I smiled. "Thanks, Mick. I really appreciate that."

"Don't start me crying yet, you two," Addison said, wrapping an arm around my waist and dabbing the corner of her eye with her fingertip. "You know I'm going to be a blubbering mess soon enough."

We sat around talking for a few minutes before my attorney, Dawson Staggs, showed up and told us we were on the one o'clock docket. Along with fifteen other cases. It was apparently standard procedure to schedule everyone at once, and you just sat around until your case was called. To our surprise, we went second.

As we all filed into the courtroom and stood before the judge's bench, we could hear some gasps as we were recognized. But honestly, I didn't care. With the exception of my wedding day, this was the best day of my life, and a few additional pictures on Facebook weren't going to ruin it for any of us.

"Mr. Hart," the judge said. "I see you are here to adopt the young man in front of me. That would be Jaxon Mitchell Bryant. Is that correct?"

"Yes, ma'am," I said, my heart thundering in my chest.

"Do you care to introduce the people you brought with you?" she asked sternly. She was probably in her late sixties with short, fluffy white hair. She was very businesslike, and I appreciated that she was making some last-minute observations before just handing Jaxon over to anyone.

"Yes, ma'am," I answered. "This is my mother, Yvette Johnson, and her husband Rick," I said, gesturing behind me to my left. "And this is Jaxon's paternal grandfather, Mitchell Bryant, and my manager and friend, Adam Roberts," I said, gesturing behind me to my right.

"It's very unusual to have a paternal grandfather in the courtroom when the child in question is being adopted by a father," she said with surprise. "And you're supportive of this adoption, Mr. Bryant?" she asked Mick.

"Yes, ma'am," he said. "Jaxon deserves to have a real dad in his life. And since Austin can't be here, Jason has proven time and time again that he's the next best thing."

She nodded. "And how do you feel about it, young man?" she asked Jaxon directly. He thought for a minute.

"My dad will always be my dad, ma'am," he said politely. "But I'm really lucky that I'm gonna get to have two dads. My teacher said some kids don't even have one."

I put my hand on Jaxon's shoulder and squeezed as I heard Addison start crying next to me. In half a second, my mother was handing her a tissue.

"You look like you're in agreement with all of this, Mrs.

Hart," the judge said. Addison just nodded, not able to get any words out, and I pulled her closer to me.

"Your home study looks good. Your background checks are clean. And it's clear you have the support of all sides of the family. Is there anything you'd like to add, Mr. Staggs?"

"Just that I've worked with a lot of adoptive parents over the years, and Mr. Hart is one of the most committed I've ever seen," my attorney replied. "There is no doubt in my mind that he will do his best to take care of this little boy, no matter what comes their way."

"Duly noted," she said. "Well then, since everything is in order, I hereby order that Jason Allen Hart is now legally the father of Jaxon Mitchell Bryant, in all that fatherhood entails. I further order that the child's name be legally changed to Jaxon Bryant Hart and will be changed on his social security card and birth certificate. Jason Hart's name will also be added to the birth certificate as the father of the child. Any objections?"

The courtroom remained quiet.

"Then it is so ordered," she said, slamming the gavel down on her desk.

And just like that, I became a father.

Chapter FOUR

When we walked into the backyard just an hour later, the party was already in full swing. You would think after spending a couple of weeks with each other for the wedding, we'd all be sick of each other. But there was nothing the Bryants and Harts loved more than a good family celebration.

Vanessa had outdone herself with decorating the back yard, and Deuce was already in full-on grill mode, complete with hot dogs, hamburgers, and brisket. It just wasn't a Texas barbecue without the brisket.

But maybe my favorite part was the twin cakes sitting side by side. They were homemade cakes and nothing fancy. What made them perfect was that Vanessa had carefully written "Welcome to the family, Jaxon" on one, and "Welcome to the family, Jason" on the other.

She nailed it. There was no separation between our families anymore. Not that there had been before. But now it was legal. And that meant the world to me.

"Hey! How'd it go?" Deuce called out over his shoulder as he cooked.

"It was great!" Jaxon said before taking off after Emma to the playscape to the left of the yard.

Deuce chuckled. "Does that kid ever calm down?"

"Never," I admitted, taking two beers out of the fridge and handing him one. "It went well, though. Didn't take nearly as long as I thought it would. I guess the hard parts were all done before the actual hearing."

"Yeah, I can't imagine them bringing a kid into the courtroom, only to say, 'Sorry, it ain't happening today,'" he said. "Did the judge approve the name stuff?"

"Yep," I said, taking a swig of my beer. "She didn't even ask about it. Just signed the paperwork and moved along."

"I'm really impressed you suggested using Bryant as his middle name," he said while flipping the burgers. "With the way that fucker cheated on Addison without even caring about her feelings, I'm not sure I would have had the stomach to honor him in any way."

"I really thought about it," I said. "But when it comes down to it, nothing about the adoption was about Addison. It was all about Jaxon. And even if I wanna kick Austin's ass for hurting Addison the way he did, I have a lot of respect for how he was as a father."

"You're a good man, Hart. Not a lot of people would see it that way." He looked around the back yard like he was searching for something. "Where's Adam, anyway?"

"Probably writing up the press release as we speak," I said, taking a swig of my beer.

"You sure he's not still avoiding Samantha?"

I chuckled. "From what I understand, he finally laid it on the line and she took it really well." I shrugged. "Go figure.

He'll be here soon. You know he wouldn't miss beer, brisket, and cake for anything."

We spent the afternoon relaxing on the patio, just hanging out and being a family. At one point, the kids decided to swim, which meant Deuce had to get in with baby Trace. Which meant I had to get in with Deuce. It was one thing to toss Jaxon around the pool, but when you added Emma to the mix, I got a pretty serious workout in.

"Jason," Jaxon said a while later, swimming up to me. "I don't feel so good."

"Come here, buddy," I said, pulling him through the water to the steps. "What's not feeling well?"

"My stomach hurts," he said as I felt his forehead.

"You're feeling kind of warm, too. You wanna come sit out with me for a while?"

"Yeah," he said with a sleepy look on his face. "Can I sit on your lap?"

I smiled. This is the part of being a parent I was gonna love. "Sure, buddy. Let's get toweled off."

We made our way over to the patio again, wrapped ourselves up, and settled into one of the overstuffed outdoor chairs.

"Hey babe," I said, interrupting Addison's conversation with Samantha and Lindsay about some latest celebrity gossip. In all actuality, I was giving Addison an out from a conversation she probably wasn't enjoying, and I knew it. "Do we have any children's Tylenol or anything?"

She stood up and walked over with concern in her eyes. "Why? What's wrong?" she asked, eyeing Jaxon, who had already fallen asleep in my arms.

"He seems warm to me and says his stomach is hurting."

"Hmm," she said, feeling his forehead. "Yvette, you took

him to the doctor while we were gone, right?"

"I sure did," my mom said as she sat down next to me, hovering over Jaxon, too. "They figured it was probably a virus. Told me to make sure he was drinking enough and getting lots of rest until he felt better."

"He's probably just having a hard time kicking it," I said as Addison went inside for a thermometer and some medicine. "We'll just make another appointment for tomorrow."

"Better make it for later in the day," Deuce said as he sat down across the table from me, his plate piled high with food. "It's almost July. Six am workouts start tomorrow morning, Jay. You've been lazy long enough. Or maybe you *haven't* been lazy," he said, waggling his eyebrows up and down and grinning like an idiot.

"Really, dude?" I reprimanded. "You're gonna say shit like that in front of my mother?" He just laughed.

"Oh, Jason," Mom jumped in. "I've been around Michael long enough to never be shocked by the things he says."

"See?" he said, giving me a pointed look. "Your mother loves me and my sense of humor."

I just rolled my eyes at him as she continued. "Besides, I expect the both of you to be making the most of your sex lives while you're young. The more testosterone you have in your youth, the faster it wears off when you're older, and you'll be headed to your monthly doctor's appointment for your prescription of Viagra. And everyone knows how much testosterone football players have."

Deuce started choking on his brisket. "Is that true?" he said in between bites with his eyes wide. "Is there any way to stop that?"

"Look it up if you don't believe me," she said with a smile.

"Vanessa!" he bellowed as he leapt up from his chair. "Where's my phone? I need to Google some shit!"

I looked over at my mom who was trying to hide a smile. "Is any of that even true, Ma?"

"Heck if I know," she said with a gleam in her eye. "But at least it got him off the topic of your sex life. I know you're married and all, but there are some things a mother doesn't need to hear about."

I roared with laughter as I watched Deuce have an animated discussion with his wife, and Vanessa rolling her eyes at the ridiculousness of it all.

Yeah. Legal ties or not, this family was solid as a rock. Weird conversations and all.

Chapter FIVE

"Did you know there is something called the 'pee-pee teepee'?" Deuce asked while spotting me on my squats a couple days later. We were in the middle of one of our pre-pre-season workouts. Deuce and I had been doing these for the last five-plus years. You didn't maintain your status as the best on the field by getting lazy once you got the contract.

After we had moved into our new neighborhood, we had convinced Deuce and Vanessa to do the same. Vanessa had been wanting out of their condo so that Trace could have a backyard to play in and close friends around, so it worked out great. It meant driving just a couple minutes every morning to the neighborhood gym instead of all the way down to the stadium.

It also meant Addison fell into the habit of going to the gym again too, which had been a goal of hers. Jaxon was up by seven every day anyway, so an eight AM boot camp class was doable for her.

She had met a nice group of women that she enjoyed hanging out with, and they had a good time. I'll admit, when I first met her twenty-five-year-old trainer, Seth, I made sure he knew she was taken. But he turned out to be a nice kid, and he really knew his stuff. He'd even given me some advice on how to adjust my own form a couple times when I was feeling too much pressure in my back.

So yeah. It was working out for us here.

"It's like an upside-down cup, like the ones you get at a water cooler? You put it over his giant baby penis when you change his diaper, so he doesn't squirt you in the face," Deuce said as he helped me get the bar on the rack and change the weight out. "Problem is, he's old enough now that he keeps yanking the damn thing off of himself when he knows he has to go. And he thinks it's funny."

"Are you sure he isn't aiming for you on purpose because you keep telling everyone how big his manhood is?" I asked as Deuce settled himself under the bar and raised it up so he could get in position for his round of squats.

"Hey, he takes after me," Deuce said as he started to squat down. "He needs to be proud of what God gave him. Someday, he's gonna make some woman very happy."

I just rolled my eyes as I counted his reps.

"Hey guys," Addison said, walking up with her phone in her hands.

"Hey baby." I gave her a quick peck just before grabbing the bar and helping Deuce re-rack it. "What's up? Aren't you supposed to be in boot camp?"

Her eyes furrowed as she answered. "I just got a weird call from the pediatrician's office. Are you guys almost done for the day?"

I looked at Deuce, who nodded. "Yeah. We just finished

up our last set. We just need to run a few miles on the treadmill and then we're done. Why? Did the doctor say something?"

"I didn't actually talk to the doctor. I talked to a scheduler of some sort. Dr. Laabs wants us to come in to discuss Jaxon's test results."

"What do you mean?" I asked as I wiped my face and neck with a towel. "Is something wrong?"

She sat down and began chewing on her lip. "I don't know. They've never done anything like this before. I asked if the doctor was going to see Jaxon and she said it wasn't necessary to bring him in. This is making me a little nervous, Jason."

I sat down next to her, put my arm around her, and squeezed her shoulder, careful not to get her all sweaty. "I'm sure it's fine, babe. She probably just doesn't want us to drag him into the office and be bored so she can tell us he's allergic to ragweed or something."

"Maybe," she said, but she didn't look convinced. "I just have a weird feeling. Do you think your mom could watch him when we go? The appointment is at ten."

"Why don't I just take him home with me?" Deuce offered as he took a swig of his water. "I'm sure Vanessa wouldn't mind having someone entertain Trace for a couple hours so she can take a breather."

"If you think she wouldn't mind, that would be great, Deuce, thanks," Addison said, still looking worried.

"Look, babe," I said. "Why don't you head to boot camp and work off some nervous energy while we get these miles knocked out, and I'll meet you outside the locker rooms at nine forty-five. The office is just around the corner, right?" She nodded. "We'll head in there, talk to the doc, and when nothing is wrong, we'll go out to lunch."

"Yeah," she said quietly. "That sounds good. You're right. I'm probably making this into a bigger deal than it is."

I smiled and kissed her temple. "Good. Now go work on that fine ass of yours and I'll see you soon," I said, smacking her rear as she stood up.

She winked at me over her shoulder as she walked away.

"You think everything's okay?" Deuce asked as we made our way over to the treadmills.

"Oh yeah," I said, sounding more confident than I felt. "I'm sure this kind of thing happens all the time."

The truth was, I was scared to death. As we started our five-mile run, I couldn't shake the feeling that something wasn't just wrong, but that nothing would ever be the same.

Two hours later, Addison and I were sitting in Dr. Laabs's office, waiting for her to come talk to us. We tried making small talk, but we were both kind of lost in our own thoughts. I kept reminding myself that this was no big deal. This kind of thing happened all the time. But that nagging feeling just wouldn't go away.

After what seemed like hours, the door finally opened and the doctor walked in.

"Hi, Addison! Nice to see you again," she said cheerfully. Dr. Laabs was a petite blonde woman, probably in her early thirties. She was wearing plain blue scrubs and a lab coat. She seemed like the kind of person Addison would be friends with if they didn't have the whole doctor/patient thing going. "You must be Jason," she said, extending her hand my direction.

"It's nice to finally meet you. Jaxon has talked a lot about you," she said as I shook her hand.

I chuckled. "I'm sure he's talked to you about a lot of things."

"Yes, he's quite the chatty Cathy, isn't he?" she said with a grin as she pulled open a medical file and began reading.

A few minutes later she started asking questions.

"So Jaxon has been complaining of tummy aches and he's been getting fevers, right?"

"Just randomly," Addison said quickly. I could tell she was nervous.

"Does he also seem fatigued?"

I laughed. "Jaxon doesn't ever get fatigued," I said.

"Unless he's feeling bad," Addison answered. "Then he'll curl up on Jason's lap and fall asleep."

Dr. Laabs nodded and stood up, coming around the desk and leaning up against it.

Taking a deep breath, she began speaking. "Here's the deal. When we drew blood the other day, we did a CBC and white blood cell count. He's anemic for sure. But his white blood cell count is also extremely high . . . just about off the charts. And his platelets are very, very low."

She stopped talking while we let that sink in for a minute.

"I'm sorry, I don't understand what you're telling us," I finally said.

"In layman's terms, he apparently has a really bad infection. However, he doesn't have any of the normal symptoms associated with an infection, no fluid in the ear, no sore throat, no upper respiratory illness. Whatever is happening is staying pretty hidden."

I looked over at Addison, whose face was drained of any normal color. "So what does that mean?" she whispered.

"That's the part that we don't know quite yet," Dr. Laabs said, crossing her arms. "I'm not going to beat around the bush or make it sound better than it is. It could very well be a really bad infection in his blood that we can't see in routine tests. Or it could be a genetic disorder, an autoimmune disease." She paused before dropping the bombshell on us. "Or it could be cancer."

I heard Addison gasp, and I grabbed her hand. This was way more serious than either of us anticipated, and I wasn't sure what to do or say. So I held on to Addison like a lifeline as I felt my entire body go numb.

"I don't want you to jump to conclusions yet," she added quickly. "I just don't want to downplay whatever is going on and have you blindsided later. I'm referring Jaxon to a hematologist/oncologist at Texas Memorial Children's Hospital. They'll run some more tests and figure out how serious this actually is. My scheduler is already working on making an appointment for him as soon as possible since this has been going on for a couple weeks now."

She stayed quiet for a few minutes as we absorbed everything she had just said.

Jaxon was going to an oncologist.

Jaxon might have cancer.

My little boy . . . my son . . . might be . . . he might be . . .

I refused to think the words as soon as they crossed my mind. My job was to protect this family, and if it took every last remaining cent I had, that's what I was determined to do.

I forced myself back into the conversation with the doctor and started firing off questions.

"What kind of test will they do there?"

"Most likely they'll draw more blood first. If they don't like the results, he'll probably have to do a bone marrow biopsy. That way they can determine exactly what's causing all of Jaxon's symptoms and what course of treatment will be the best options."

"What is the likelihood that it's actually cancer?"

"That's a hard question to answer. Ninety percent of the time when a patient's counts appear out of control like it is, it indicates some form cancer. But I don't want you to get ahead of yourselves. There are still several other things it could be. You don't want to rule anything out just yet."

"But no matter what, there is something serious going on that will need to be treated?"

She paused at that question. "Mr. Hart . . . Jason, Jaxon is very sick. So far, we've been lucky that he's only displayed these symptoms for a few weeks, which means we've caught it, whatever it is, relatively early. But short answer . . . yes. Something serious is going on, and you are probably in for a long haul."

I looked over at Addison, who was white as a sheet and staring off into space. "Baby," I said, turning in my seat to look at her straight on. "Baby, look at me."

She slowly turned to look at me, and I saw the tears in her eyes. "Jason," she whispered. "I can't lose my baby boy. I just can't . . ." And that's when her tears started falling.

I pulled her to me and sat her on my lap while she wept. I could practically feel her fear. I was feeling the exact same way.

"We're gonna do everything we can, baby," I whispered into her hair. "I just got him. He's not going anywhere. He's just not."

Dr. Laabs remained silent as Addison got out all of the excess emotion she was feeling. Once she was calm, had cleaned her face with a tissue, and was sitting back in her chair, Dr. Laabs answered the rest of our questions. There weren't many. Without a diagnosis or a treatment plan, there wasn't a lot she could tell us. After just a few minutes, it became clear that Dr. Laabs was only the first stop in what may have been a long line of doctors.

We drove in silence to Deuce's house. While I wasn't sure what to say to Jax, I had this overwhelming urge to be near him. I didn't want him at Deuce's house, I wanted him home with me. It was a stupid feeling. It wasn't like I could protect him from some random disease that was inside his body. But that didn't mean my protective instinct was any less strong.

I drove up the long driveway and put my truck in park.

"I think we should tell Deuce and Vanessa," I said, still looking out the windshield.

"Why?"

I took a breath and turned to look at my wife. "Because I don't feel like we should tell anyone else yet. My mom will freak out and want to spend all her time at the house. I don't trust Samantha not to blast it all over social media before we're ready. And no telling what Mick will do. Deuce and Vanessa already know something's up," I said, nodding my head toward their front door. "And even if it's not today, we're going to need to vent a little while we're still waiting. Not to mention, we could need more babysitting. We might as well be honest with them."

She sighed and nodded her head. "I agree. And they'll give us some space. I'm not really ready to have our family bombard us quite yet. We're gonna need them later on. And I kind of just want to be . . . I don't know . . ."

"You want it to be just *us* for a few more days."

"Yeah," she said, looking back over at me with more tears

in her eyes. "I'm not ready to let go of my fairytale life just yet."

I grabbed her hand and kissed her knuckles. "It's going to be okay, Addison," I said, my voice wavering a bit as more emotion swept through me. "I know money can't buy health. But if we have to, we'll pay for whatever treatments he needs —the best doctors and medicines available. If this is all my contract is for, I'll do my damnedest to make as much money as I can for as long as he needs it."

She reached up to cup my cheek with her free hand and wipe a tear that had slid down my face. "I know, baby. I know you will. Because you are the best daddy Jaxon could ever ask for."

I kissed her knuckles again. "Come on. Let's get this over with," I said as I turned to open the truck door.

"Wait!" Addison said quickly. "What are we going to tell Jaxon?"

I stopped and turned back around to look at her. "The simplest answer that makes any sense. I'm not sure what a fallback answer would be this time, though."

I jumped out of the truck and ran around to let her out too. When I grabbed her hand and led her up the front steps, I could feel her shaking. As I rang the doorbell, I wondered if I was shaking, too. I was full of so many weird feelings, I just couldn't tell.

Deuce opened the door with his characteristic ornery smile on his face. "Hey! You lovebirds decided against going to lunch, I see!" As he looked at our faces, his expression fell. "What the hell is wrong?"

"Where are the boys?" I asked as we stepped inside the foyer.

"In the playroom, making towers and knocking them

over," he said, shutting the door behind us. "*What's wrong?*"

I sighed. "Where's Vanessa?" Addison asked. "We need to talk to you guys."

Deuce went to get Vanessa as Addison and I made our way over to the kitchen table. Deuce's house was about two thousand square feet larger than ours. He wasn't trying to keep up with the Jones's or anything. He was just really impulsive when he got excited, and according to Vanessa, he got really excited when they toured this house. Personally, I thought it was way too big, but it was Deuce's money. And Deuce's problem.

"Hey guys," Vanessa said as she made her way into the kitchen and sat down warily. "I just turned a movie on for the boys, so they should be entertained for a while. And you guys don't look so good."

Deuce handed me a beer and Addison a Dr. Pepper as he sat down. He knew us well.

As Addison sighed, I grabbed her hand and launched into the details of everything we had just learned. When I was done, Deuce sat back and crossed his arms.

"Of course, we're here for anything you need," Vanessa said. "Is there anything we can do right now?"

Addison looked up and smiled at her. "Honestly, right now we just want to spend the next couple of days wrapping our brains around everything. We're not telling our families until we know more."

"Were they able to set an appointment yet?" Vanessa asked.

"Yep," Addison nodded. "Friday morning at Texas Memorial Children's."

"Well, we're here for whatever you need," Vanessa added. "No matter what the diagnosis."

"Thanks, Vanessa," Addison added.

"I think you need to give Adam a heads up," Deuce interjected. "Didn't he say you picked up three new sponsors the other day?"

I nodded.

"He may need to be ready to reschedule some of those photo and commercial shoots. And to be ready for anything the press throws his way. You know how quickly stuff like this can get out," Deuce added.

I nodded again. He was right. Working with sponsors didn't take up as much time as football did. But it still took several hours at a time. If I needed to be at any of Jaxon's appointments, and I really felt like I needed to be, my schedule was going to need to be arranged carefully.

Just then, Jaxon came barreling into the room.

"Jason! Mom! You're back!" he exclaimed as he flew into my arms with a smile on his face. I immediately changed my expression and forced myself to look happy. "Did you have fun at the doctor? What did she say?"

"She just said we need to take you to another doctor to figure out what's going on," I answered, trying to stay with the simplest answer I could come up with.

"How come? Is she not smart enough to figure it out?" he asked seriously.

I smirked. "Nah. Apparently you've stumped her, buddy."

"Oh. Okay. Can we get some pizza on the way home?" he asked, switching gears quickly. "Trace slobbered all over my snacks before he fell asleep."

"Of course," I said, ruffling his hair. "Why don't you go grab your shoes and we'll head out."

"'K," he answered as he bounded away.

I turned to Addison. "How was that for simplest answer

and hope for the best?"

She smiled at me and grabbed my hand. "Well done, Dad. I think you're getting the hang of it."

Chapter Six

The day of Jaxon's bone marrow biopsy, I'd thought it was one of the worst things that could happen.

I was wrong. So, so wrong.

Don't misunderstand . . . that day was awful. Of course, the second round of intense blood work didn't show anything we didn't already know. So, while Addison and I anxiously sat in the parents' waiting room, Jaxon had a gigantic needle shoved into his hip bone so they could get some bone marrow out of him. Sure, they gave him laughing gas since he had to be awake for the procedure, for whatever reason. But he still cried and kept asking us to take him home after it was over. It was miserable.

But that was nothing compared to the overwhelming anxiety of this day, because this day we were finding out the diagnosis and all our treatment options.

Addison and I were ushered into a giant conference room, where it seemed like dozens of people were already waiting for us, including Adam and Judy, the team PR representative.

I looked over at Addison, who seemed to be thinking the same thing I was . . . This many people in the room wasn't a good sign.

A stout, redheaded woman stood up and came toward us.

"Mr. and Mrs. Hart, my name is Debbie Benton," she said, introducing herself and shaking our hands. "I'm going to be Jaxon's nurse practitioner. Won't you have a seat and we'll make introductions."

Addison and I took a seat by Adam and looked around. Fortunately, Adam came prepared and had a notebook in front of him. I had no idea how much of the information we were about to get was going to be retained, and I had been too nervous to even think about it until now.

"I'm going to quickly introduce everyone to you," Debbie said once we were settled in. "We don't expect you to remember everyone's names today, but everyone here will be on Jaxon's diagnostic team."

Jaxon's diagnostic team. He didn't even have an official diagnosis yet, and he already had a diagnostic team? Being in this room already felt surreal.

"This is Dr. Don Bates," she said, gesturing to a man in a white lab coat sitting next to her. "He is Jaxon's new pediatric oncologist. He's head of the department and is one of the best oncologists in the country." She then gestured to the woman on her right and continued around the table. "This is Kristina Lowe, Jaxon's research nurse; Elizabeth Dalton, Child Life Specialist; and Ruth Davis, head of the hospital's PR department."

"Why does the hospital's PR department need to be involved?" Addison asked

Debbie smiled at her kindly. "We'll explain all that in a minute. But first, I know you guys have been waiting for the results of Jaxon's bone marrow biopsy."

We nodded nervously, and I grabbed Addison's hand.

"Dr. Bates can give us more information on what they found," Debbie said, once again gesturing toward the doctor and then sitting back in her chair as he took over the conversation.

Dr. Bates appeared to be in his mid-forties or so. His dark hair was thinning on top, and he looked tired. He spoke as he glanced down at a medical file in front of him. "Mr. and Mrs. Hart, when Jaxon's white blood count was done, it was extremely high, which, of course, indicated an infection of some sort. It was just a matter of figuring out what, exactly, it was."

I could feel myself holding my breath as he spoke.

"The part of the puzzle we looked for is a certain type of white blood cell called neutrophils. His neutrophil count was about three hundred, which is well below where it should be. That led us to the bone marrow biopsy to determine what kind of infection is causing all of his symptoms." He looked away from his file and took his glasses off, looking at us directly. "In short, Jaxon has what's known as Acute Lymphoblastic Leukemia. It's essentially a cancer of the blood. In fact, it's one of the most common forms of cancer in children. But it is still cancer."

At that point, my head fell forward and just hung there in defeat. I felt Adam squeeze my shoulder and heard Addison's soft cries next to me. I wanted to reach over and hug her, comfort her. But I was frozen to my chair, thoughts swirling around in my brain.

My son has cancer.

My *son* has cancer.

My *son* has *cancer*.

I felt like I was in a dream. Surely none of this was real.

Surely I was going to wake up any minute and it would have been one big nightmare.

At that moment, I had to move. I jumped up from my chair and just started pacing and taking deep breaths, trying desperately to hold myself together. Every once in a while, I'd turn around and look at the doctor, ready to ask a question. Then I'd lose my train of thought and start pacing and breathing again.

I was vaguely aware of Addison being quietly comforted by Judy, but I was so wrapped up in such intense emotions that I couldn't seem to do anything about it.

The room remained quiet as Addison and I processed what we had just been told. After a few minutes, I finally felt like I could ask the one question I wasn't really sure I wanted the answer to. "Okay, doc," I said, hands on my hips, feeling like I could hyperventilate at any moment. "Give it to us straight. What are his chances?"

I felt myself holding my breath as I waited for what could possibly be even worse news.

"The cure rate for this particular leukemia is over ninety percent," he answered. "Of course, we're going to need to be aggressive in our treatments. But I'd say, of all the cancers he could have gotten, Jaxon has the most curable one."

Ninety percent, I kept thinking. *Ninety percent cure rate. That means only ten percent don't make it. No, don't think about that. Focus on the ninety percent. We'll get Jax some chemo. We'll kick this cancer to the curb.*

Holy shit, my son has cancer.

My thoughts were all over the place. The statistics should have made me feel better, but statistics are hard to think about when your kid has a life-threatening illness. Statistics are just numbers that some scientist or mathematician looks at after your child's outcome is final. Statistics aren't your child's face and your child's laugh and your child's hugs. Statistics are supposed to give you hope. And as much as I wanted to hold on to that, I was still trying to wrap my brain around the diagnosis.

After a few more minutes of pacing, Adam stood up and came over to me, stopping me mid pace.

"Hey man," he said, putting his hands on my shoulders. "It's a lot to take in. But we need to find out what the treatment plans are and where we go from here. You need to focus on what he said, okay? Jaxon is strong and resilient. He's gonna beat this. There's a whole team of people here to help Jaxon. But we've gotta hear the game plan, okay?" I nodded and felt his hand squeeze my neck. "Come sit back down so we can get all the details worked out. I'm writing everything down, and we'll make this as easy on you guys as possible."

I nodded again and sat back down, looking over at Addison.

"You okay?" she asked.

"No," I answered. "You?"

"No," she said. "Let's just get this over with."

"Okay," I said, turning back around to the table. I expected to see looks of pity. But there weren't any. There was compassion, sure, but there was also resolve. At that moment, I could see that this team was determined to save Jaxon's life, and they believed they would accomplish their goal. The least I could do was listen to how they were going to do it.

"So what's the plan, doc?" I asked, opening up the conversation again.

He gave me a compassionate smile and began detailing the treatment plan. "Jaxon is going to need four to six weeks of an intense chemo regimen to beat the leukemia. We've scheduled for him to be admitted in forty-eight hours. That will give you guys time to wrap some things up at home and get him mentally prepared to be admitted. The day after he comes in, we have him scheduled to have surgery, where we'll implant a port into the large central vein in his chest."

I felt my eyes go wide at that statement. But Adam didn't miss a beat.

"What is that for?" he asked.

"A port-a-cath, or port as it's commonly called, is a device that gives us easy access to his large central veins for his chemotherapy," Dr. Bates explained. "This way we just numb the area around the port every day and use a small needle to give him the meds instead of having to use a large needle and find those veins every day. It's much less intrusive for the patient and safer for us."

"Will he get to go home during his treatment?" Adam asked. I was glad he jumped in with all these questions. I couldn't think of anything to ask, but I knew I would have thought of it later.

"He'll live here at the hospital for the duration of his treatment," Dr. Bates answered. I heard a gasp next to me, presumably from Addison. "He'll have his own private room on the wing, and you both are welcome to stay with him the entire time. The chair reclines into a cot-sized bed. It's not as comfy as home, but it keeps you right next to him the whole time if you choose to stay."

"I'm supposed to report to training camp in California in just over a week," I said, looking at Adam. "What am I . . . ? How do we . . . ?" My brain couldn't even figure out what it was trying to ask. Fortunately, Adam understood.

"First things first, man. Let's do this first. Then we can sit down with the coaches and discuss your schedule if we need to, okay?"

"Okay," I said, turning back to face the front.

"What about school?" Addison asked. "Will he be able to start school next month? He can't miss that much school or he'll be held back."

The child life specialist, I couldn't remember her name, jumped into the conversation. "The timing of his treatments really works in our favor on that end, because if all goes well, he'll only miss a couple of weeks, if that. If not, however, the schools typically will provide a tutor while the kids are in the hospital. The tutor will come every other day to ensure he doesn't fall behind. We also have a small computer lab on the floor where the school-aged kids can get on the same websites their teachers use and log into the same pages their friends are on. We find it helps keep the kids' spirits up when they can still compete with their friends on things like "First in Math."

I heard Adam's pen scratching furiously on his paper as he wrote things down when the doctor jumped back in.

"Initially, we'll start him on a regimen of four separate drugs, all through an IV or his port. Vincristine and L-Asparaginase are both forms of chemo to kill the blood cells in his body, thereby killing the leukemia. He'll also be on Doxorubicin to help fight off the cancer cells. And Prednisone is the steroid we'll be using to help suppress his immune system, so we can better control the leukemia cells. That's one of the big reasons he'll stay in the hospital," he explained. "Once his immune system is down, he'll be highly susceptible to any form of illness and that can be very, very dangerous."

"What if the drugs don't work?" Addison asked. I was surprised she could think enough to ask questions. I still couldn't figure out how to stop my brain from swirling around in my head.

"That's where I come in," said another person, whose name I didn't remember. "My name is Kristina, and I'm Jaxon's research nurse." I was glad she reminded us of her name. I hoped everyone would do that for a while. "I'll work with Dr. Bates to keep close tabs on how the medicines are working. I report any unusual results to the FDA for research purposes."

"Wait, we're using research drugs on Jaxon?" Adam asked.

"All drugs remain under the watch of researchers when they're on the market," Kristina said. "That's why you'll see some drugs used widespread for a few years and then disappear. We also enroll all kids with cancer in the trials, strictly to gather the data on how well the drugs are working. The long-term side effects are always being watched and monitored to ensure the benefits outweigh the risks, and to determine which ones have better long-term results. It's how cancer treatments are constantly improving."

Makes sense, I thought.

"But that also means I keep tabs on which drugs are known for which particular side effects. If Jaxon can't tolerate one drug well because, for example, it gives him a rash, we won't switch to another drug that has that same potential side effect, that type of thing. So his regimen will be tailored to his specific situation."

"I know I'm not the parent, I'm just the friend," Adam said, "but I feel like you've really thought of everything."

Debbie, the nurse practitioner, smiled as she spoke. "We're one of the best pediatric oncology hospitals in the country for a reason. We take what we do very seriously and recognize that no two bodies are alike. No two people are going to respond the same to every treatment. The key is figuring out which one works the best for the individual. Which leads us to a pretty critical part of our meeting," she said, looking over at the final person in the room, who hadn't said anything yet. "I already introduced you to Ruth Davis with hospital PR. We call her in when we're treating a more high-profile patient."

I wanted to groan. Through this entire nightmare, it had never even occurred to me that the hospital would have to bring their own public relations department into it.

"I've already gotten security up to speed on the situation," Ruth said. She was a small woman with short brown hair and black-rimmed glasses. She was probably in her thirties and appeared extremely professional. "At this point, very few people have put together that Jaxon Hart is Jason Hart's newly adopted son." She actually used her fingers as quotes when she said my name. I guess it was a way to differentiate Jason Hart, the pro football player, from Jason Hart, the father. "We still need another day to ensure all the details are set in place. But rest assured, we have extremely strict guidelines for our employees to adhere to, and HIPAA guidelines are no joke."

"What's HIPAA?" I asked.

"It's the law that protects patients from their private medical information being exposed publicly," Ruth answered. "We take it very seriously around here. But rest assured, if those policies are broken by any of our employees, they will be terminated immediately and won't qualify for unemployment benefits. They all know this."

"What's the plan for when the press finds out?" Adam asked, still writing furiously.

"That really depends on how you want to handle it," Ruth said. "Obviously they won't be allowed into the hospital without prior authorization. We can go as far as holding a press conference. Or we can do something like issuing a press release. Or we can wait for them to start calling and use our standard media response answer."

"Which is?" Adam prodded.

"HIPAA laws prohibit us from disclosing information on whether or not *anyone* is a patient. We are not willing, nor able, to confirm or deny whether or not Mr. Hart, or anyone else, is admitted here at this time," she spat out, without missing a beat. I admit, I was impressed with how quickly it rolled off her tongue. I had no doubt she had used that answer on a regular basis.

Adam turned to Addison and me. "What do you guys think?"

"Can I voice my opinion?" Judy, the team PR manager, asked.

We both nodded.

"First of all, Jason, Addison, I know your heads are spinning right now, so I hope you'll trust Adam and me on this particular issue. It'll be one less thing for you to think about." Addison and I both nodded. "My thoughts are, you guys know how ruthless the press can be around here. I don't think you'll be able to keep this out of the news for very long, if at all," she said matter-of-factly. "Second, Jason, your fans really are some of the most loyal I've ever seen in all my years of working for this team. I think you'd be surprised how many people you'll find will start praying for Jaxon to get better as soon as they hear the details from you. And right now, he needs all the prayers he can get."

I looked at Addison to gauge her reaction. She looked around like she was sorting through her thoughts before she spoke up softly.

"I hate admitting it," she said to me, "but she's right. There's nothing we can do about the obnoxious fans. But the really good ones, the ones who have been nothing but kind and supportive, deserve to hear it from us. And I'm willing to accept whatever prayers and well wishes they want to send our way."

I smiled at her. She had come so far from the woman who would do anything to stay out of view of the press. "Plus, I trust them," she added. "Judy's right. There's too much to think about. Figure out when the news needs to break, but let's leave the rest to them on this issue."

I looked back at Adam. "Let's start with a press release. I don't want too many details of his diagnosis going out. I'm okay with the type of cancer, but not what his treatments entail or anything." Adam nodded as I continued, finally feeling like I had some sort of control over the situation. "I'd like to wait a few days until it goes out. We obviously need to tell Jaxon and our family. Judy, who knows on the team so far?"

"No one, yet," she said. "I'm also bound by HIPAA laws, and since pre-season doesn't start for another couple weeks, it's still pretty quiet around the office. Everyone is already heading up to Oxnard to set up for training camp."

"Okay," I said. "I'd like to have a sit down with Coach tomorrow and give him a heads up and see what we can work out. Obviously, I'm under contract, so I have to keep working. But maybe they'll let me fly back and forth on our off days. It's gonna be rough with me not being here for his entire treatment, but maybe I can watch all the team plays on my laptop from the hospital room or something, I don't know." I rubbed my hand down my face, feeling overwhelmed already, and we'd only been dealing with cancer for ten minutes. I had no idea how we were going to get through this.

"I'll give your sponsors a heads-up that there are some personal things happening and your schedule is going to be tighter than normal for a while," Adam said. "I'll see how many of those we can get done as soon as we get back from Cali so we can try to free up some of your afternoons and evenings. Will that work for you, Addison?"

She nodded. "I appreciate you trying to rearrange things, Adam. Hopefully it'll just be for the next four weeks, right?" she asked, looking hopefully at Dr. Bates.

"That's exactly what we're hoping for," he answered. "I've had several patients who go through one four-week treatment only to go straight into remission, never to get cancer again."

"Then that's what we're going to shoot for," I said, feeling for the first time that not only was this team determined, but between all of us, we may actually reach this goal faster than I initially thought.

Chapter Seven

"It was so nice of you two to have all of us over tonight," my mom said as she finished up the grilled salmon we had just finished eating. When Addison first brought up the idea of having salmon for our "party," I thought there was no way it would fill me up. But after the day we'd had, I had virtually no appetite anyway. At least salmon went down without much chewing required.

"Where are Deuce and Vanessa tonight?" Mom added.

"They offered to babysit Jax so we could have an adults-only get-together," Addison said as she began clearing plates off the table.

"What about Adam?" Samantha quickly added. From what he'd told me, Adam had made it clear to Samantha that there was never going to be anything between them when they got back from the wedding. She wasn't taking it hard or anything. But she was still flirty whenever he was around. That was Samantha, never giving up hope on love, or some shit like that.

"He had a ton of work to do tonight," I said as I began piling dirty dishes on top of each other for easier transport.

"So it's just the family tonight?" my mom asked. "Those two men definitely keep things from getting too serious. I feel like we're having a family meeting or something."

I locked eyes with Addison as she came back into the room. She had obviously heard what my mom had said. I took a deep breath and steeled myself for the upcoming conversation.

"We kind of are, Ma."

All eyes turned to me as Addison stopped with the dishes and sat down.

"What's going on, Jason?" Mick asked.

"You okay?" I asked Addison quietly before addressing everyone else. She just nodded. I smiled at her before turning back to the faces of our family. "The doctors figured out why Jaxon keeps having fevers and tummy aches."

No one said a word, but you could see the concern on their faces. So I continued.

"His white blood cell count is extremely high, so he was referred to a hematologist/oncologist who did some extra blood work and a bone marrow biopsy on him last week. We got the results today."

I paused one more time, giving everyone time to digest everything I was saying.

I finally spit out the words I could never take back. "Jaxon has leukemia."

"What?"

"Ohmygod."

"Cancer? Are they sure?"

Everyone started mumbling at once.

"They're sure," I added. "It's called Acute Lymphoblastic

Leukemia, or ALL. It's the most common form of childhood cancer and has a really high cure rate. But yeah. He has cancer."

The room went silent for a few seconds before my mother finally spoke up. "So what's going to happen now?" Her husband Rick reached his arm around her and started rubbing her back, her voice starting to sound a bit hysterical. "Do they have a plan yet?"

"You should have seen it, Ma. They have a whole team of people specifically for Jaxon," I said, smiling over at Addison, who looked as pleased with our medical team as I was. "He's being admitted for treatment day after tomorrow. And he'll be there for a while."

"What does 'a while' mean?" Mick asked.

"Four to six weeks."

Mick groaned and set his elbows on the table, face in his hands.

"We've had a few days to get prepared for this news, so it's not as shocking to us as it is to you all," Addison said. "And as hard as it was to hear the diagnosis and treatment plan today, we seem to have a really, really good team on our side."

"Who is the doctor?" Rick asked. "I had a friend who worked at Texas Memorial. I assume that's where he's going?"

Addison nodded. "The doctor's name is Don Bates. He's the head of the department and is supposed to be really good."

"Oh yeah, I've heard of him," Rick said. "He's been listed as one of the nation's best in several magazines. I'm so glad he's the one assigned to his case."

"Well, I think this is one time when that celebrity status comes in handy," Addison said as she turned to look at me, squeezing my hand. "I have a suspicion they are going to go the extra mile to ensure a good outcome."

Suddenly, Mick pushed away from the table. "I can't lose my grandson, too! I won't!" he said as he slammed his fist down on the table. Then he stormed out of the room, and we heard him exit out the back.

We all looked at each other, startled but not terribly surprised by his outburst.

"He'll be okay," Samantha said quietly. "Just give him a few minutes to absorb it all."

"So what do you need us to do to help out?" Mom asked. Leave it to her to immediately go into mama bear mode.

Addison and I looked at each other and shrugged. "We don't really know yet," Addison replied. "Obviously Jason has to keep working, which means training camp in a week. The only thing I can anticipate needing help with is someone to bring me some real food when Jason is gone. I don't plan on leaving that hospital until Jaxon does, and I can't imagine hospital food is all that great." She chuckled. "It's weird some of the details you start to think about when you're in this situation. I mean, who cares about hospital food when your son is . . . when he has . . . oh god . . ." And just like that, she finally broke down and started sobbing.

Before I could even get my arms around her, my mom swooped in and was hugging and rocking her, tears running down her own face.

"It's gonna be alright, Addison," she said soothingly, rubbing her back. "I know this is scary and overwhelming, but that little boy is strong. He's smart. He's stubborn. If anyone can kick this, it's him. We're just gonna keep praying for the best outcome possible and believe that he will be just fine."

Addison nodded and finally pulled away, wiping her tears with her fingers. "Sorry about that." She sniffed. "We've been so busy, I haven't had a chance to just get it out, ya know?"

"Never apologize for crying for your baby," Mom said, petting Addison's hair. "Especially not in a situation like this. But don't you worry. There are quite a few of us who will jump at the chance to help you out. Even stay with him while you get errands done. There is no reason for this to disrupt your lives any more than necessary with so many of us here to help relieve some of the pressure."

Addison smiled at her and took a deep breath before sitting back into my arms.

"We really need everyone to be careful to stay healthy, too. Especially if you plan on going to the hospital," I added. "If you feel a cold coming on, grab that Airborne or some Vitamin C or something. And make sure all your immunizations are up to date. He can't have sick people around him."

"Consider it done," Mom answered for everyone.

"And please keep this under wraps for now," Addison said. "We haven't even told Jax yet. Adam is working with Judy and the hospital to come up with the official press release for when it's time. But we'd like Jax to get settled into his routine before all the crazy starts. That means no social media about it, Samantha."

Samantha quirked an eyebrow at Addison. "I may love my Instagram, but even I know this is a private family matter. I'll stick with cute selfies, thank you very much."

Addison smirked. "I'm sure you will."

We settled into silence as we all went back to our thoughts. Addison finally spoke up. "Should I go talk to Mick?"

"Maybe I should. You know how us guys are about emotional shit," I said as I kissed her on the temple and stood up. I grabbed a couple beers from the kitchen before heading out the back door.

Mick was sitting in one of the lounge chairs by the pool, staring straight into the water. I walked up next to him and put my hand out. "Beer?" I said as I sat down on the lounge chair next to his.

He looked over at my outstretched hand and paused for just a second before taking the bottle. "Thanks," he said quietly, twisting the top off and taking a swig.

We sat in silence for a few minutes before Mick finally spoke up.

"I thought losing Austin was the worst thing that could happen in my life, ya know?" he said, still staring at the water. "A father is not supposed to outlive his son. It's just not natural. But this . . . this is just too much. I can't outlive my grandson, too. It's too much," he said as he choked back a sob. Once he gained control, he continued. "Austin was a grown man. He had lived his life. It wasn't a full, complete life, but he was an adult. Jaxon is just a little boy. He's just a baby. I can't lose him, too." The sobs started coming, and I sat there quietly, letting Mick process his grief. I'd be lying if I said I didn't shed a few tears as well as we sat there. The entire situation was heartbreaking on so many levels. For me. For my wife. For my son. For the other members of our family. I wasn't just sad because I was sad. I was also sad for them. And that just made it so much worse.

After a few minutes, he calmed down again. When he took another swig of his beer, I spoke up.

"You know, Mick, I have been shell-shocked by this whole thing. I keep feeling like I've failed them both. I know that's dumb, because there's nothing any of us could have done. But I feel like I *should* have done something, ya know what I mean?" I asked as I turned towards him. He nodded in understanding.

"I went into that meeting today knowing there was a ninety percent chance we were getting a cancer diagnosis. Ninety percent! It may as well have been a guarantee. It was the most hopeless I think I've ever felt in my life. Even worse than when my dad died." I began peeling the label off my beer bottle, just to give my hands something to do.

"But it was the strangest thing. There were five hospital staff members, two football staff members, and Addison and me in that meeting. You should have seen it. As soon as they told us what was happening, they had a detailed plan in place. Everything from when he's being admitted to what meds he's taking to multiple back-up plans in case they don't work. They even have security ready with extra measures, and my coach doesn't even know what's happening yet." I looked over at Mick again.

"By the time the meeting was over, I realized if anyone can save Jaxon's life, it's this group of people. They are a well-oiled machine already. All we have to do is work with them. I mean, his chances are so, so good. Doesn't change the fact that it's cancer. But it gave me this glimmer of hope that everything is going to be okay. I'm still struggling with the 'what ifs', mind you. But there is hope. It's all I have to hold on to, but that's what I have to do."

I sighed, hoping I wasn't going to start shedding tears again. After a few minutes, Mick finally looked up from the water.

"I trust you, Jason," he said. "You love that boy as if he were your own flesh and blood. I know that. If you say you believe this team is the one that can cure him, then I have to trust that."

I nodded in agreement.

I wasn't kidding when I said that glimmer of hope was the

only thing getting me through without completely falling apart. But now that the whole family was on board, at least we could hang on to each other, too.

Chapter EIGHT

I drove back from my meeting with Coach Ramiro feeling just a little bit stronger now that I had the support of my team as well. Sure, the entire team didn't know as of yet, but I knew Coach was on the phone right now with all the team owners and the entire coaching staff, filling them in on Jaxon's diagnosis. We were just going to continue doing things the way we always did them, with some adjustments here and there as needed. And he had no problem with me flying back and forth on our off days, which meant I'd have about one day a week at home. It was better than nothing.

In the event that Jaxon took a turn for the worse—just the thought made me shudder—they would have Mason Hayes ready to go. It was pretty normal procedure to have the second string ready to back us up, but I knew Mason would be worked extra hard this season and would be given extra time to mesh with the first string players. There were no guarantees with chemo, and the team needed to be prepared for me to break my contract if necessary.

But I wasn't going to think about that. The cancer wasn't going to get that far. That's what I was choosing to believe.

Besides, I had mentally prepared myself to finally tell Jaxon what was going on. Normally the hospital staff would be with us when we told him, so they could answer any questions he had, but we opted to do this alone. We had to tie up a bunch of loose ends before his month-long hospital stay and really wanted to tell him together. This was our first chance.

I took a deep breath when I drove up the driveway. I thought it was bad telling the family what was going on. But this . . . this was on a whole new level.

Would he understand? Would he ask questions I couldn't answer? Would he be worried and scared? What do we say if he asked if he was going to die?

This was one of those times when the simplest answer wouldn't be enough. And "because I told you so" wouldn't cut it either. This was the side of being a parent that everyone dreads. And here I was, right smack in the middle of it. Totally unprepared for what was coming.

When I walked in through the garage and tossed my keys on the desk, I saw Addison baking cookies.

"What are you doing?" I asked as I stood behind her, putting my hands on her waist and kissing the top of her head.

She was using a spatula to move the warm cookies onto some wax paper. Considering the amount of dough she had left, I assumed she was preparing to feed a small army.

"I decided that if we have to stay there for a month, we're going to need some chocolate chip cookies with us," she said quietly, keeping an eye on the family room to make sure Jaxon wasn't eavesdropping. He wasn't. He was too engrossed in Minecraft again to be listening. "Just a comfort from home we can bring with us. How did your meeting go, anyway?" she asked as she turned her head toward me for a quick kiss.

"Fine," I said, giving her a peck and making my way to the fridge for a glass of milk. Can't have cookies without milk, and there were enough for her to spare a few. "He's getting everyone up to speed. He's good with me flying back and forth as long as the treatments are going okay. I told them I'd give them a heads up if there are any significant changes. Otherwise, we're just all going to keep in our normal training routines. We've still got a week until I have to report to California, so hopefully we'll know more by then."

"Know more what?" Jaxon asked as he walked into the room and sat down on a barstool. "You made a lot of cookies, Mom! Can I have one?"

"Sure," she said as I reached into the cabinet for another glass. If I couldn't have cookies without milk, neither could my son.

"What are they for, anyway?" he asked as he took a big bite. "Is there a bake sale or something for the school?"

We looked at each other, and I shrugged my shoulders. "Now is as good of a time as any," I encouraged her.

With a deep breath, Addison put down the spoon she was using the put fresh dough on the sheet and wiped her hands off on a hand towel.

"Remember the bone marrow biopsy you did last week?" she asked him calmly.

"How can I forget," he said as he took another big bite. "I still have a giant bruise on my butt. I bumped it when I was swimming at Deuce's house yesterday. It really hurt!"

I smiled at his innocence in the whole situation. It wasn't exactly an appropriate time to smile, but he wasn't worried about a biopsy. He was worried about a bruise. I hoped he would feel the same way about the rest of this conversation.

"The biopsy gave us the information we needed to figure out why you keep having tummy aches and fevers," Addison said.

"Yeah? So what's the matter with me?" he asked as he took a big drink of his milk. "Aahhhh," he said with a look of contentment on his face as he put the glass down. He obviously didn't understand the seriousness of the situation at all.

"Jaxon, honey," she said softly. "You have leukemia. Do you know what that is?"

He shook his head "no" and took another bite of his cookie.

"It's a kind of cancer."

He swallowed his bite and thought for a minute before speaking again. "Didn't the teacher at my school have cancer last year? Mrs. Jefferson?"

"She did," Addison confirmed.

"But she's okay now," he added.

"She is."

He took another bite and got lost in his thoughts again. "She had to have a lot of medicine that made her hair fall out to make her better."

"The medicine was part of a treatment called chemotherapy."

"Am I going to have chemo . . . what's it called again?"

"Chemotherapy."

"Yeah, that. Am I going to have that?"

Addison looked over at me, so I stepped in.

"Yeah, bud," I said. "Tomorrow morning we're taking you down to the hospital where you're going to get your own room so you can get chemotherapy."

"Are they gonna use another giant needle on me?" he asked, eyes wide. "I don't want them to do that again! That hurt!"

"No," I said. "They're gonna put you to sleep and do a little surgery to put what's called a port right here in your chest so they can just numb it and use a tiny needle for the medicine," I said, rubbing my own chest to show where it would go.

"Oh," he said, thinking hard and taking another bite of his cookie. Once he swallowed, he started asking questions again.

"How long will I be there?"

"Probably a month."

"A month!" he exclaimed, his jaw and eyes wide open.

"Your mom and I aren't going to leave you there by yourself," I added quickly, trying to reassure him. "We're allowed to spend the night and everything so you don't have to worry about that."

"But what about school?"

"I'm sorry, bud, you won't be able to start with everyone else."

"I don't have to go to school?"

I was starting to wonder exactly what Jaxon was thinking. He didn't seem as upset as I thought he would. "You'll have a tutor that comes in a few times a week to make sure you don't fall behind."

"Can I play Minecraft at the hospital?"

I narrowed my eyes and crossed my arms, letting him know I was on to him. "Yesssss."

"And will there be other kids there to play with?"

"Uh huh."

"Cool," he said, and he jumped up off his stool and headed back to the family room. I looked over at Addison, who had a dumbfounded look on her face.

"Did that just happen?" Addison asked me.

"I'm gonna guess he doesn't understand the gravity of the situation quite yet," I said with a laugh.

Addison just shook her head in disbelief and went back to baking cookies. "Ya know, we could try to force the situation, but I think I'd rather let him keep his innocence for a little while longer."

"I couldn't agree more."

I kissed her and headed toward the family room to get my ass beat on the Xbox.

Chapter NINE

We made our way down to Texas Memorial Children's Hospital the next morning. Two days ago, I would have expected the mood to be somber. Instead, Jaxon was chatting a mile a minute about the frog he found at recess last year and how loud his teacher screamed when he brought it in the class to show her.

I looked over at Addison and smiled. It was a little weird to be smiling on our way to chemotherapy, but it was better than the overwhelming grief we had been feeling.

Adam and Ruth met us at the valet parking and took us straight up to the oncology wing. It was different from what I expected. The walls were all painted bright colors. The ceiling tiles were all obviously decorated by kids. There was even a giant fish tank embedded in one of the main walls.

As we walked by a main room, we saw a bunch of children hanging out, talking and laughing and playing games. Some of them were bald. Some in wheelchairs. Some dragging IV poles behind them. But every single one of them was smiling. And I had never seen so many toys in my life. It was not at all what I had expected to find in a hospital wing full of kids that were fighting cancer. It didn't seem to be a sad place at all.

Once we got to his room, Jaxon immediately ran to the window and looked out.

"Look how high up we are, Mom!" he exclaimed excitedly.

Adam just snickered. "I take it he doesn't quite get it?"

"That's pretty normal," Ruth said with a smile. "It's hard enough for adults to wrap their brains around all of it. Can you imagine trying to figure it out as a child?"

"He's just excited about not having to go back to school next month," Addison said.

"Most kids are," Ruth answered. "But that's okay. We want the hospital to be a fun place for them and not a scary place. So we let them treat it like they're on vacation. The better their spirits are, the better their chances are."

I looked down at Addison and put my arm around her shoulder, kissing her temple. "Maybe it'll help keep your spirits up too."

"Maybe," she said, nuzzling into my chest. We had been doing that a lot lately. Touching and nuzzling and just generally sticking close together. I guess we needed the comfort from each other.

"Well, hello there, Hart family," said a loud cheery voice behind us. I turned to see Dr. Bates walking into the room with a giant bow tie on and a clown nose. I could feel my brow furrow in confusion. "Well, you must be Jaxon," he said, walking over to the window and shaking Jax's hand. "I'm your new doctor, Dr. Bates. How ya feeling?"

Jaxon looked him up and down once. "You're my doctor?"

"Sure am," he replied.

"Then why are you wearing a clown costume?" Jaxon asked with some skepticism to his voice. Adam snickered off to the side.

"Well just 'cause we're at the hospital doesn't mean we can't have any fun," Dr. Bates said.

Jaxon thought again for a second before shrugging his shoulders. "Okay."

"Would you mind hopping up on your bed for me, Jaxon?" Dr. Bates asked. As he said it, there was a small knock on the door and a pretty young nurse walked in the room. She had short, light-brown hair and a wide, welcoming smile. She was really cute, which meant Jaxon was gonna love her.

"This is Bri," Ruth said, introducing us. "Debbie is the nurse practitioner, but Bri will be Jaxon's daytime nurse for the next several weeks. She's one of our best, and we thought her personality might mesh well with Jaxon's."

"It's nice to meet you," Bri said before turning to Jaxon without sparing us another glance. "Hi Jaxon. I'm Bri, your nurse."

"Hi Bri. How come you aren't wearing a clown costume too?" he asked.

She laughed. "Only the doctors get to wear the clown costumes around here," she said with a smile. "They get to have all the fun. But don't worry," she whispered. "I know where the squirt guns are."

Jaxon's face lit up like Christmas when she said that, and I knew she had won him over.

"We still have to finish up some admission paperwork and go over the press release," Ruth said. "Do you guys feel comfortable leaving Jaxon in Bri's care for a few minutes?"

I looked at Addison and shrugged. "Sure," Addison said. "Hey Jaxon, we're gonna be right back. We have to go do some paperwork, okay?"

He barely answered as he waved us away. "Looks like he already has a crush on his hot nurse," I whispered in Addison's ear as we left the room. She smiled while smacking me on the chest with the back of her hand.

"Well, what do you think so far?" Ruth asked when we finally made it to her office and sat down.

"So far he's happy, which is great," Addison said. "I know the treatment isn't going to be fun, but I love that no one is trying to make him be all serious about the situation."

Ruth smiled. "That's a really common misconception. People automatically assume the oncology ward in a children's hospital is a sad place. And there is a lot of sadness at certain times. But these are still children. And naturally, children are joyful, positive creatures. I hope you'll be pleasantly surprised by how much laughter you'll hear."

Addison smiled up at me. "I hope so too."

"Okay, so, Addison," Ruth said, getting back to business. "I want to go over the press release with Jason and Adam, so if you don't mind working on the admission paperwork, we can get you guys back to your son as soon as possible."

"That's fine," Addison said, picking up a pen and turning her focus to the stack of papers now in her hand.

"I have a tentative press release typed up, Jason," Ruth said. "But I wanted to run it by you and Adam first and talk about when we want to release it."

I looked over at Adam. "You wanna do the honors? See how close it is to what we talked about the other day."

"Sure," Adam said, reaching for the paper Ruth was handing him. It took him less than a minute to read through it and assess it. "It looks a lot like what we wrote up on our end, Jay. Just that Jax has ALL. His prognosis looks good, and we have a great medical team working with him. Please pray for a full recovery, etcetera. Looks good to me."

"So this works for you, then, Jason?" Ruth clarified with me.

"If Adam says it's fine, it's fine," I answered. "He's been doing this so long for me that I'm fine with you discussing things like press releases with him."

Ruth nodded. "Good. That'll make it easier on everyone. So when do you want this released?"

Addison looked up from her paperwork. "Is it possible to wait until the rumors start circulating? Eventually someone is going to talk about Jason coming in and out every day. But maybe we'll get lucky and it'll be a few days."

"I'm okay with that if you guys are," I said to Adam and Ruth. They both nodded.

"I'll keep tabs on everything and let you know when I start hearing things, Jay, so you won't be blindsided. Then I'll let you know, Ruth, and we can release them at the same time," Adam said, going right into manager mode.

"That's perfect," she agreed. "And if I start getting phone calls from the press before then, I'll give you a call, Adam, and we can discuss a game plan."

Once we worked out the logistics and Addison finished the paperwork, we trekked back down the hall to Jaxon's room. A hall I'm sure we would become very familiar with over the coming weeks.

"Mom! Jason!" Jaxon said excitedly as Bri tried to take his blood pressure. "Can I go to camp this year? There's this really cool camp and only kids who have cancer are allowed to go and they ride horses and swim and stay in cabins and do campouts! Can I go? Please?"

I chuckled. "What are you talking about Jax?" I asked as I sat down in one of the chairs by his bed. Addison went to the bags and started unpacking into the dresser up against the wall. She always liked to feel settled when we stayed somewhere besides home.

"What's it called again?" he asked Bri, who was logging something on a laptop. Probably his blood pressure results.

She smiled at Jaxon before looking at me. "It's called Camp HopesALot," she said while wrapping up the blood pressure cuff and securing it to the stand. "It's a pediatric oncology camp about forty-five minutes North of here, and it's a blast. I volunteer there every summer."

"See?" Jaxon said. "It's a real thing and even Bri gets to go! Can I go? Please?"

I looked at Addison, who just smiled at me and rolled her eyes. Lately we'd been tag teaming on his exuberant ideas, so I was on my own.

"Tell ya what," I said, stretching my legs out. "Let's get through chemo, see how you're doing when next summer comes, and if all looks well, we'll look into it and see how to get you involved. Will that work?"

"Yes!" Jaxon exclaimed, throwing his fist in the air. Apparently he still hadn't figured out that "maybe" didn't mean "yes."

Bri just smiled as she started toward the door. "I'll leave you guys to settle in. If you need anything, just call the number on the white board right there. It'll get you directly to me. I'll come check on you soon, Jax."

"Don't forget the squirt guns!" he yelled after her.

"Well, looks like we've got some time to kill, buddy," I said. "What do you want to do?"

He thought for a minute. "Minecraft."

I just shook my head. The boy had a one-track mind sometimes.

Chapter TEN

I handed my keys to the valet as I stepped on the curb in front of the hospital a few days later. It was nice not having to walk through the parking lot—kept me more incognito. My time at the hospital was limited, so I didn't want to have to stop for autographs and pictures. I didn't want to be rude either, though.

"Jason Hart." I heard the familiar voice behind me as I walked through the doors, holding on to my hat as I walked through the doors so the blast of the air conditioner wouldn't blow it off.

I stopped and turned around, a look of annoyance on my face. "April," I replied. "What can I do for you."

It wasn't a question as much as a challenge. April Gill from Channel 5 News had been a thorn in my side for years. She was notorious for digging up private information and spewing it all over the local news and Internet. I had hoped that once I got married, she would lay off me, but no such luck, I guess.

"Oh, I just wanted to make sure everything was alright," she said, feigning concern. "Word on the street is you've been here a lot over the past few days."

"Uh huh," I deadpanned. "And that's a story because. . .?"

"I didn't say I was after a story," she said with mock offense. "I was just making sure everything was alright with your new family and all."

"Thanks," I said, turning from her and pressing the up button on the elevator. "I appreciate your concern, but everything is just fine." I knew she was going to find out the truth eventually, but I wasn't going to confirm anything to her.

"Tell that new wife of yours I said hello," April said with a smile as the doors to the elevator opened and I stepped on. I ignored her and headed straight to the back wall to let others on as well. I waited until the door closed and April was out of my sight before asking to have the button to floor three pushed. I knew it wouldn't throw her off the trail, but it might slow her down a bit.

When I got off the elevator, I pulled out my phone and headed straight to the small family restroom on my right and shut the door.

I quickly dialed Adam's number and waited for him to pick up, still jarred from my run-in with April.

"Hey, man! How's it going?" I could hear him crunching in my ear. I swear he was always eating when I called.

"It's time, dude." I knew he would know exactly what I was talking about. "I ran into April Gill outside the hospital, and she's sniffing for a story."

"Oh, shit."

"Yep." I nodded even though he couldn't see me. "I know we were hoping to wait a few more days before we went public, but at this point I'd rather make sure everyone else gets the story before she does."

"Hell yeah!" he said in agreement. "So do you want me to send the press release to all the stations except Channel 5? I can send them out now and wait to send hers until all the 5:00 newscasts have started."

I chuckled. I knew it probably wasn't right to purposely try and screw over a reporter for doing her job, but it wasn't the job that bothered me. It was how she went about it and how many times she had intentionally tried to screw over my family and my friends. I just didn't have any more patience for it this time around.

"That sounds great, man. Make sure Judy and Ruth are on board with what the plan is before they get bombarded with phone calls. And that security is ready to go."

"I'm on it."

"Thanks. Let me know if you need anything from us."

"Will do," he said, sounding like he was taking a gulp of his drink. "Go take care of your kid. You leave in just a few days."

We hung up as I headed out the door and down the hall.

Today was Jaxon's first day of chemo, and while I wanted to be there for it, I was late because of work responsibilities. One day in and we already had to shuffle things around.

I knocked on Jaxon's door and stuck my head in. "Hey buddy, how's it going?"

I walked in and leaned over the recliner, giving Addison a kiss.

"Gross," Jaxon said, barely looking up from his video game. "Why do you have to kiss all the time?"

"To show your mom I love her," I said, sitting down in the empty chair next to his bed.

"Can't you just shake hands or something?"

I chuckled. "Sorry, dude. That's not the way it works. Just close your eyes next time."

He grunted and went back to ignoring us and building some tree house or hotel or something. Who knows? No matter how many times I played it, I would never understand that game.

"How's it really going?" I asked Addison, reaching out to hold her hand and play with her fingers.

"So far, so good," she said with a shrug. "He's only been on the meds for about an hour. But I'm hopeful so far."

I looked over at Jax and saw that the port-a-cath wasn't being used yet. "Are they using the IV this time?"

"I guess so," she said. "I didn't really ask why he needed the port if they weren't going to use it today. But I'm sure they'll explain it all later."

"Gotcha." We sat, watching Jaxon play for a few minutes. I didn't realize how boring it could be when someone gets chemo. There's not a lot of action to it. You just . . . sit there. If I had realized this was what it would be like, I'd have brought a playbook to study. I'd have to remember that for next time.

"So I ran into April Gill downstairs."

Addison grimaced at the name. "I don't know what it is about us that is so fascinating to her, but I wish she'd stop fishing for stories all the time." She shifted in her seat, giving me her undivided attention. "What did she say?"

I shrugged. "The usual crap. Fed me a bunch of bullshit about being concerned as to why I've been here over the last couple of days."

"Wait," she said, holding her hand up for me to stop. "She knows you've been here for a couple days?"

"Yep." I nodded slowly. "I guess I wasn't doing as good

of a job staying anonymous as I thought."

Addison groaned. "I was really hoping for a few more days of quiet before the crazy began."

"I know," I said sympathetically. "I went ahead and gave Adam the go-ahead to send the press release to everyone except Channel 5."

Addison's jaw dropped. "You did not!" She giggled. "You're so bad!"

"What?" I asked, smiling at her. "They'll get it at 5:01 pm. After everyone else has already scooped them on the story."

Addison's shoulders shook with laughter. "I'd like to say that was rude, but she so deserves it."

I waggled my eyebrows up and down. "That's the point."

"Hey Mom," Jaxon said, pausing his game. I looked over at him and realized his face was looking pale all of a sudden, and he was leaning back on his pillows like he couldn't hold himself up anymore. "I don't feel so good."

As Addison jumped up, Jaxon leaned over and puked all over my lap.

"Incoming call from . . . Lindsay," my hands-free device said as I drove home to change. It had never occurred to me that I would need to bring extra clothes when I was at the hospital. And none of the scrubs Bri offered me fit. Lengthwise they were okay, but I couldn't fit my thighs in the leg holes. So here I was, driving home in puked-on shorts so I could change before heading back.

I pressed the button to pick up the call.

"Hey Lindsay," I said as I changed lanes on the highway.

"What. The. Fudge," she said slowly.

"Haha! Mommy, you said a bad word!" I heard Emma yelling in the background and giggling up a storm.

"I said fudge, Honey," Lindsay responded in her mother voice. "Fudge isn't a bad word. It's a dessert."

"What the fudge, what the fudge," Emma started yelling.

I chuckled as I listened to Lindsay try to get her to be quiet. Finally, she had Emma calm and started talking to me again.

"Sorry about that," she said calmly.

"I don't ever want you to complain that I'm a bad influence again, Lindsay. Clearly it is all your doing," I joked.

"Uh huh. I don't want to talk about that, Jason. I am really mad at you."

"What? Why? What did I do?"

"Why am I finding out *from the radio* that Jaxon has cancer!"

"Uggghhh," I groaned. "I am so sorry, Lindsay. It completely slipped my mind to call you."

"But you could call the local media?"

"I'm sorry. That was the press release that Adam and the hospital issued today. We weren't going to say anything yet, but April Gill was sniffing around, so we went ahead and let the other stations scoop her."

"Ew. That woman makes my skin crawl." No one in my inner circle was a fan of April's. "I'm not done being mad at you, but I need to know what's really happening. Not just what some press release says."

I spent the next couple of minutes catching her up to speed, telling her everything the doctor had said about the diagnosis and treatment and answering all her questions.

"So today was his first day of chemo?" she finally asked.

"Yep."

"How's it going so far?"

"Well, it was going fine for a while. And then he got sick and puked all over me."

She roared with laughter. "That's what you get for not telling me! It's called 'karma.'"

"Oh, I will never forget again," I said, laughing with her. "Not after this."

"Do you guys need anything at this point?" she asked when she stopped laughing, getting back to the conversation.

"I don't think so," I said, trying to think if there was anything that could be done yet. "You may need to call my mom and ask her. I'm sure she's got a spreadsheet and meal plans ready to go for when I head to training camp later this week."

"Oh god, I forgot about training camp. So you are gonna be gone for a month."

"Pretty much. They'll let me fly home on my off days to check in and give Addison a break. But yeah. It's gonna be rough."

"I'll call your mom then and make sure she puts me on all her call lists."

"Okay."

"And don't worry about picking up the school paperwork next month. I'll pick everything up that you guys need to fill out and help Addison with it while you're gone so we can get the tutoring process started if we need it."

"You already know about that?" I asked, surprised she didn't have to research anything or call her boss to find out what to do.

"Sadly, Jaxon isn't the first kiddo I've worked with to have chemo." She sighed.

"Yeah? How's the other kid doing now?" I asked out of curiosity.

She was silent for a moment. "He fought for about two years. But, um . . . he didn't make it, in the end."

I paused, stunned at her words.

"Jason," she said. "Stop. He was never as strong and active as Jaxon. I don't for one second expect the same outcome. It wasn't even the same kind of cancer. He had a very aggressive form of non-Hodgkin's Lymphoma. So whatever is happening in your brain, just stop."

I nodded. Then I realized she couldn't see me. "Yeah. I hear ya. Hey, listen, I'm pulling up to my driveway now, so I need to let you go, okay?"

"Okay," she said, sounding sad. "Seriously, Jason. Call me if you need me. I'm right here, and I can take Addison anything she needs when you're gone."

"Thanks, Lin. I appreciate it," I said before disconnecting the call.

My mood was completely different now. Sure, it was fun to pull one over on April Gill. And it was fine to joke about Jaxon puking on me.

But the reality of the situation had just hit me again.

And the truth was, it wasn't a fun reality. No matter how many good moments you could find in the middle of it.

Chapter ELEVEN

A couple days after his treatment started, I would have gladly gotten my ass kicked at Minecraft if it meant Jaxon would stop throwing up.

His chemo was brutal. Everyone was working on finding a different drug to put him on that wouldn't have such bad side effects, but weren't having much luck so far. Apparently finding a cancer medicine that *doesn't* have nausea as a side effect was damn near impossible. And for some reason, the anti-nausea meds weren't helping.

When he wasn't throwing up, Jaxon was just lying in bed, sleeping or staring off into space. He had resorted to staring at Minecraft videos on YouTube instead of playing his favorite game. His lips were chapped, and he had dark circles under his eyes. His hair hadn't started falling out yet, but I was terrified that whenever I ran my hand through it, I'd end up pulling it out. And we were only two days into the actual treatment! Dr. Bates assured us that it was normal for some children to react more strongly than others, but that with the exception of the obvious, nothing was wrong or unusual. Jax was just one of the unlucky ones.

For the most part, Addison was trying to take it all in stride, but I could tell it was wearing on her. She hadn't left Jaxon's bedside since we got here, not even to shower, so I finally kicked her out. Told her to go home, clean up, and take a nap. She swore she didn't need it, but when our child life specialist, Elizabeth, got involved and reminded Addison that we had at least three and a half long weeks ahead of us, most of it with me out of town, she finally agreed to go. But only as long as I stayed with him. That was a no-brainer. Of course I was staying with him.

Deuce and I were still meeting up in the mornings to work out, but that was the extent of the work I'd done. Adam had kept his word, though, and starting the next day I'd have to do several photo shoots and commercials for my sponsors. I didn't normally mind them—it was part of the job I'd gotten used to—but with Jax so sick, the timing was terrible.

Three hours after Addison had left, Jaxon finally stopped throwing up. He fell asleep, and I needed a break. I stepped just outside the room and slid down the wall until I was sitting with my arms resting on my knees. With my head back and eyes closed, I heard someone slide down the wall and sit a few feet away from me.

I looked up and saw a man about my age, dirty blond hair and dark circles under his eyes, sitting in the same position I was. Only he was staring at the floor.

"Long day?" I asked, just making conversation.

He half smirked, half grimaced. "You have no idea."

"I take it your kid's having a rough go of it like mine, huh?"

"Yep," he said, still staring at the floor. "What's your diagnosis?" he finally asked after a few minutes of silence.

I sighed. I hadn't told anyone outside my family and my coach. Part of me wanted to tell him it wasn't any of his business. The other part of me was just glad to finally meet someone in the same situation as me. "ALL. You?"

"Brain tumor," he answered.

"What stage?" I asked out of curiosity.

"Stage four. Terminal," he said, with almost no inflection to his voice.

My jaw dropped, and I looked straight ahead, trying to figure out how to respond to that news. I knew Jaxon was bad off, but I couldn't even imagine what stage four terminal cancer would be like. I suddenly felt grateful for the extra vomiting we were experiencing. "I don't know what to say, man. That really sucks."

"Yeah," he said.

We sat quietly for a few minutes before he looked over at me. "She's only two, man. Two years old. She never even got a chance. What the fuck is that? How the hell does that even happen?"

"I don't know," I answered honestly.

"I've been trying to wrap my brain around all of this," he continued. "And I can see how it happens to adults, ya know? We're stupid. We smoke and drink and eat like shit. But kids . . . kids haven't done anything wrong. My baby girl didn't even get a chance," he said softly, tears starting to roll down his face.

Another few minutes of silence went by. I just sat there quietly, letting him do what he needed to do. I couldn't imagine what he was going through, so I wasn't gonna judge, and I wasn't gonna try to find words to fix it. He finally spoke again.

"I'm sorry, man," he said, wiping the tears off his face

with the back of his hand. "I shouldn't have unloaded this on you."

"Hey, don't worry about it," I said. "I get where you're coming from. I mean, I don't get stage four, and I hope I don't ever have to. But the whole idea of cancer is just a mind fuck. We've only been here for four days, and it's already overwhelming."

He smirked. "Yeah, it's overwhelming all right."

"Where's her mom?" I asked. "Are you doing this by yourself?" Normally I wouldn't be asking such personal questions, but something about being strangers in the hall with dying children made it okay to ask and answer things you normally wouldn't. Kind of like when you're on an airplane and you know you'll never see the person again. I guess this was my first experience with supporting another parent like I had heard happens here.

"She's at work," he said. "Iris has been here for a few months, and with her being so young, we just don't feel comfortable leaving her alone at all. So my wife works the day shift, I work the night shift, and we switch off being here. That way Iris is never alone."

"Why doesn't one of you just quit your job for a while?"

He snickered.

"I'm sorry, man," I backpedaled. "I'm not trying to be nosy. Just curious I guess."

"It's okay. Nothing our families haven't already asked us. The answer is easy: medical bills. Insurance is only an eighty-twenty split with a cap at a million dollars."

"Wait, what do you mean by a cap?" I knew we were different from the average family at the hospital because of my job, but I was just now beginning to understand how far removed we really were from the average person.

"The insurance will only pay up to a million dollars of Iris's medical expenses. Once we hit that cap, they don't pay anymore. At all. She's been here for four months *this time,* which means paying for the room, doctors, anesthesiologists, medicines. Not to mention parking, gas to get here, and meals. Add that to the bills from the last three hospitalizations. And then there are regular expenses so we don't lose the house. So I work to pay our household bills, and my wife works to pay all the medical expenses. Otherwise, we could end up bankrupt on top of everything else."

"Aren't there any special programs or something that can help pay for everything?"

"We don't qualify," he answered. "We have insurance and make too much money. I'm sure there's something out there, but so far we haven't found one we qualify for yet."

"Ohmygod," I said softly, rubbing my hand over my face. I had no idea this type of thing happened to people. It seemed so unfair. I wanted to do something about it, help somehow. But what could I do, besides pay his bills for him, and I wasn't in a position to suggest something like that.

"I'm Roger, by the way," he said, sticking his hand out.

"Jason," I said as I shook it.

"Yeah, I know who you are," he said, standing up and wiping off the back of his pants. "I used to have season tickets. Section 134. Loved going to games with the guys."

"Maybe someday you'll get to come out again. Just enjoy a beer and get to relax."

"Maybe," he said with a shrug. "Anyway, I'd better head back inside before she wakes up. Good talking to you."

"You, too," I said. "Good luck."

Somehow, though, I didn't believe luck was going to cut it for Roger and his family.

Chapter TWELVE

It is amazing what a couple of weeks and the right combination of meds can do for a kid. After a messy start, it seemed the medical team had finally found exactly what Jaxon needed to fight the leukemia, without making him throw up every minute of the day. He still felt like crap. There was no avoiding that part. But he had enough energy to play his video games and crack some jokes. He had even ventured to the giant playroom a few times and made friends with a couple of kids his age.

I wouldn't say the experience was fun for any of us. But we were grateful to be over the constant sickness.

Addison and I were spending my day off waiting in Dr. Bates's office. While Jax had been in surgery having his port put in place, Addison, Mick and I had some blood drawn to see if we were potential bone marrow matches for him.

Today was the day we'd find out the results. I knew the likelihood of me being a match was slim, but I was still hopeful. And if not, chances were better for Mick to match, and even better with Addison.

Addison put her hand on my knee. "Stop," she said.

"What?" I asked absentmindedly.

"You're shaking your knee."

"I am?" I asked, turning to look at her.

"Yes. It's making me nervous."

"Sorry. I'm just . . ." I started and then trailed off.

"Yeah. Me too."

"Addison," I said. "Look at me." She looked up at me with her beautiful hazel eyes. I could see how the last six weeks had taken a toll on her. She looked more tired than I'd ever seen her. I wondered if I looked the same way. "It's gonna be okay."

She tried to smile at my words but never quite made it. "It will be. Somehow."

I hated not being able to fix this for her. For Jaxon. For all of us. I'd never felt so helpless. It seemed like all we ever did was sit and wait. Wait for lab results. Wait to see how Jax would respond to different treatments. Wait for doctors to come talk to us. I got a reprieve every time I got on that airplane to go back to work. I got to focus my energy on something else. But Addison did it day in and day out. All the time. Without any breaks, because I wasn't here to help her, and she flat out refused anyone else who offered. I was worried, not just about her physical health, but about her mental and emotional well-being as well. At some point, I was afraid she'd crack, and I didn't know how to stop it.

After another few minutes of silence, wrapped up in our own thoughts, Dr. Bates finally walked in.

"Jason, Addison," he said, looking at a medical chart as he walked around to sit behind his desk. "Good to see you again."

"You too, Dr. Bates," Addison said politely.

"I see Jaxon is doing pretty well with his treatments now that we've finally found a combination that doesn't make him so sick," he said, clasping his hands and leaning forward on his desk.

"Um, so far so good," Addison replied, glancing over at me. "It helps that everyone at the hospital is so friendly and fun. Kind of makes us forget why we're there sometimes."

"We like it that way," Dr. Bates said with a smile. "We prefer to focus on their life rather than the possibility of death."

"It's certainly more tolerable that way," Addison agreed.

"That it is," Dr. Bates said, looking down at the medical chart again. "So the results of your testing are in."

I felt Addison go stiff next to me. I grabbed her hand and squeezed.

"Jason," he said, "it's not a huge surprise that you're not a match. The chances of a non-biological parent being a bone marrow match are the same as it would be with a stranger. But we all knew that going into this."

"Yeah, I know." I sighed with defeat. "You can't blame me for hoping, though."

"Of course not," he agreed. "Addison, your results are also in. Unfortunately, you're not a match either."

I put my arm around Addison's shoulder as her head dropped in disappointment and Dr. Bates let us absorb the news.

"I'm assuming Mick didn't match either?" I finally asked, rubbing Addison's back.

"Unfortunately not," he said, sitting back in his chair.

"So what does this mean?" Addison asked.

"Well," he said, leaning back in his chair and steepling

his fingers. "It means we continue to wait for the bone marrow registry to find a match. New candidates come in every day, so there's always that possibility. We have a bit of time. There's no definite that he's even going to need a transplant. He's responding well to the chemo, and I'm hopeful he'll be in remission within the next couple of weeks."

"So wait," I said, confused. "So we don't even really need a bone marrow donor?"

"That's hard to predict, Jason," he said. "The thing about leukemia is that you can respond really well to the treatments one day and the next, they just stop working. We like to have a donor lined up as quickly as possible because if a patient takes a turn for the worst, we won't have the time to look for one. We'll need one immediately. Bone marrow transplants are kind of our last resort."

"Why?" I asked, still rubbing Addison's back. "I mean, why don't we just do it and knock it all out at once?"

"Just like any treatment, a bone marrow transplant has lots of side effects. Many of them can be severe and most are long term. Infertility, eye disease, autoimmune disease . . . It's not a decision to take lightly."

"Ohmygod," I said, putting my elbows on my knees and dropping my head in my hands. "So if it gets to that point, we have to choose between letting him die, or letting him live a life with all these things that could happen. What kind of decision is that?"

"Unfortunately, it's a decision that has to be made more often than I like," he said. "But rest assured, it's not an option we take lightly. We make sure it is the absolute last resort before we even pitch the idea to you."

I looked over at Addison, who had stayed quiet through the entire exchange. "You okay, babe?"

She sighed. "I'm just . . . absorbing everything. There's always so much to think about."

"There's more," Dr. Bates said, causing us both to look back over at him. "Although, I have to say, this is news I've never had to deliver before."

I sat up straight and took a deep breath.

"Addison, since you were the most likely candidate, when we drew your blood, we went ahead and started doing the normal screenings to make sure your blood was clean. It turns out, even if you had been a match, we couldn't allow you to donate."

My entire body ran cold. There's no way I could take more bad news. Not now. Not while Jax was fighting for his life.

"Why not?" Addison asked in a whisper.

"Addison," Dr. Bates said with a smile. "As it turns out, you're pregnant."

My jaw dropped, and I lost all thought.

"Pregnant," Addison said, confirming what we had just heard.

"Yep," he said, looking at that chart again. "From the looks of your hCG levels, I'd say you're about ten weeks or so along already."

"Ten weeks?" she said more loudly. "How is that possible?"

Addison continued to banter back and forth with the doctor about girl stuff that I didn't care to know about while I counted backwards in my head. Then it hit me and I started laughing.

"What's so funny?" she asked me with some obvious irritation in her voice.

"Ten weeks ago, to the day, was our wedding day, Addison," I said with a laugh as I remembered her riding me while wearing her wedding dress.

"Why are you laughing, Jason?" she asked. "This isn't exactly funny news, considering the circumstances."

"I'm sorry, babe," I said, still chuckling. "But I told you cutting me off before the wedding was a bad idea! You just made my boys a better shot!"

"Ohmygod," Addison groaned. "I can't believe you just said that."

I laughed again when I heard Dr. Bates cough, trying to stifle a chuckle.

"Okay, okay," I said with my hands up defensively. "We'll talk about this in a little bit." I turned back to Dr. Bates, grateful that the ominous mood in the room had completely lifted. "So then, what do we need to do now, Doc? Not about Addison. About Jaxon."

"Well, start spreading the word. The more people you can get to test as a potential match, the better the odds are of finding a donor."

"Okay, we'll start making some calls," I said.

"And Addison, we've got a great OB department here," he said. "I know it's a hike to get to the other part of the hospital, but it might be nice to deliver here since you know so much of the staff already and you know your way around."

"Thank you," she said, standing up, still looking a little shell-shocked.

I stood up with her, and we turned to go.

"Oh," he said, causing us to turn back around. "And congratulations. I know these aren't ideal circumstances, but it's always nice to have something to celebrate in times like this."

Addison nodded as I grinned at the doctor. It was painfully obvious I was way more excited about this news than she was by the big grin on my face. But I couldn't help it. We were having a baby.

My baby.

No home study was going to have to approve it.

No judge was going to have to legalize it.

I was gonna be a dad from the beginning this time.

I'd be there for all the firsts.

And I couldn't wait.

The drive home was quiet, both of us lost in our thoughts. We were going to eat a quick lunch before we had to relieve my mom at Jax's bedside, but I also wanted to know where Addison was at with all of this. I hadn't been able to tell at the hospital. And I certainly couldn't tell now.

I threw my keys on the desk in the kitchen when we walked in, and I just watched Addison until I couldn't take it anymore.

"Addison," I said, leaning against the counter and trying to get her attention. She was flitting around the kitchen, gathering lunch supplies, trying her hardest to ignore me. So I tried again. "Addison, we can't ignore this, and I leave tomorrow morning. So we kind of need to talk about it now."

"What's there to talk about, Jason?" she asked while slathering mayo on some bread, still avoiding looking at me. "We're having a baby."

"Uh huh. And how are you feeling about that?"

She stilled for a minute then continued on with her task, but never answered. I walked toward her, grabbed the knife out of her hand, and put it on the counter next to us before turning her to me. She still wouldn't look in my eyes.

"Babe, why won't you talk to me?" I asked, tipping her chin up and forcing eye contact. That's when I saw the tears in her eyes.

"Because I feel really guilty about how I feel right now, and I'm ashamed for you to know."

Of all the answers she could have said, that was not what I expected. "So I'm guessing happy isn't the right answer?"

She snorted and turned back to the sandwiches. "You really want to know?"

"I really do."

"You realize you may think I'm the worst person, worst mother in the world when I tell you."

"I doubt that, but try me."

She whirled around and started talking faster than I had heard in a long time. It could only be described as word vomit. "I don't want to have a baby. The thought of having another child to care for right now makes me want to puke. I don't want to be pregnant. I don't want to give birth. I don't want to have a newborn. I don't want to give up what little life I have left during all this mess. I don't want anything to do with this. And yet I feel so guilty because it's *your* baby. It's *our* baby. You deserve to experience everything about fatherhood from the very beginning. And if our life were different right now, I'd be so happy. But I don't know how to have a football star husband who is away at training camp, let alone in the middle of the season, a son with leukemia, *and* a baby. It's too much. I can't do it. But I don't have a choice, and I'm stuck, and it sucks, and I just don't want this." Once again, she turned back to the sandwiches, leaving me to try to absorb everything she'd just said.

"Look." She sighed as she sliced a tomato, "I'll be excited

when the baby's here. I'll be happy and will love him and all that stuff. But I'm so overwhelmed, it's gonna take me a minute to wrap my brain around everything."

"Hey," I said gently as I pulled her back against me. "Hey, look at me." She finally relented and turned around, looking me right in the eyes. She didn't just sound overwhelmed, she looked it. "You are exhausted. You have been at the hospital almost non-stop for a month. Everything is out of our control right now, but if you don't want this baby, I mean, we have options and stuff."

"Don't even go there," she retorted quickly. "I appreciate that you would be willing to entertain options for the sake of making me feeling better for a few minutes, but you know that's not happening."

I sighed with relief. "I'm really glad to hear you say that. I know you're really upset right now, but I'm so excited I can hardly stand it," I said with a smile.

"I know," she said, cupping my face with her hands. "You haven't stopped smiling since Dr. Bates told us. Just do me a favor."

"Anything," I said, kissing her softly.

"Just . . . be excited for both of us for a while. I'll wrap my brain around it eventually. I just need some time."

"Oh, I can do that," I said, still giving her gentle pecks. "Can I ask you another question?"

"Sure," she said in between kisses.

"When can I tell Deuce what a good shot I am?" She paused mid-kiss and started laughing.

"Like I could stop you and Deuce from comparing penis sizes if I wanted to." She turned back to the counter, still chuckling, and finished making lunch.

Pregnant and in my kitchen. The Neanderthal in me was thrilled.

Chapter THIRTEEN

Thank God for the wonders of modern technology, because it sucked being away from home for a whole month when your kid was sick and your wife was pregnant.

Scratch that. It just sucked being away from home for a whole month.

I used to love training camp. And in all honesty, I still loved the workouts and reviewing the plays and studying the tapes. I loved building the camaraderie with my teammates and running drills until we wanted to pass out on the field. I still loved my job. I just wished my job was closer to home this time of year.

So here I was, FaceTiming my family from my hotel room while they sat next to each other in Jaxon's hospital bed.

"How are you feeling, bud?" I asked Jax. "You're looking a little better than yesterday."

"I feel a little better," he answered, fidgeting with some Legos he was building. If he wasn't tinkering with something, he would be fidgeting, so it was always best to just let him tinker. "I went to the playroom today and played with that kid, Jonah."

"Yeah? What did you guys do?"

"Played Minecraft."

I snorted. I should have known the answer before I bothered asking.

"And then we played some game called Sorry," he continued. "I totally kicked his butt."

"Glad to hear you're finally playing some real games," I said smiling. "I used to whip my mom at Sorry all the time."

Jaxon looked up at the screen to make eye contact with me. "You know she let you win, right?"

"What?" I asked, pretending to be offended. "I won fair and square. I was great at Sorry!"

"No, Jason." His head was shaking back and forth, looking at me like he was pitying my ignorance. "She totally let you win. She told me so."

Addison put her hand over her mouth and giggled at this admission.

"Oh, you think that's funny, do you?" I asked her with a smile on my face.

"Yeah. Kind of funny," she agreed.

"What else is going on, babe?"

"Same as always," she answered. "Chemo, naps, nurses, playrooms, crappy hospital food. Be glad you're there. We're getting bored around here."

"And the food sucks," Jaxon interjected. I would have loved to say something fatherly like, "It's not so bad," but he was right—the hospital food did suck. Instead, I went back to the question we asked daily.

"How are his counts?"

"Good," Addison said. "Dr. Bates said he's making great

progress, and it looks like we may be quickly moving toward remission."

I felt myself smile really big. "That is the best news I've heard in the last couple of weeks." Addison just rolled her eyes, knowing what I was getting at. "So, shall we continue sharing good news and tell him, babe?"

"Tell me what?" Jaxon asked without even looking up from his Legos.

Addison and I had debated when to tell Jaxon about the baby. With everything happening, we wanted to wait until Addison had gotten safely to that twelve-week point. And we wanted to wait until Jaxon had a little more strength. It appeared we had finally met both milestones, so I was getting antsy.

"Do you want to tell him, Addison? Or should I?" I asked.

"Oh, don't let me hold you back, baby," she said to me with a smirk. "I know it's been killing you to sit on this information for the last couple of weeks."

The woman knew me so well.

I took a deep breath, excited to finally let Jaxon in on the secret. "Jaxon," I started as Addison disappeared from the camera view, "Well, it seems that we are going to be adding a baby to our family."

Jaxon's head popped up and his jaw dropped open. His expression was priceless as he looked from me, to Addison, who sat back down on the bed again, back to me, back to Addison, to her stomach, back to me . . .

I wanted to laugh, but I was too busy waiting to hear what he had to say about it. Finally, he regained his ability to speak.

"You're having a baby, Mom?" he asked Addison, who just smiled and nodded. "So I'm gonna be a big brother?"

"You are," I said.

Jaxon launched himself into Addison's arms, and for the umpteenth time, I wished I were in that room with them for this moment. Instead, I watched quietly as Jaxon pulled away and Addison showed him the picture from the recent ultrasound we'd had done. I had a copy sitting on the desk right next to my monitor, so I knew exactly what he was seeing. It looked like a little alien, but it was our little alien, and my heart swelled every time I saw the picture.

When I had finally fessed up to Deuce about the pregnancy, he'd congratulated me with a manly hug and then said, "Welcome to the pussy side, where grown-ass men tear up at a picture of a tiny blob." He hadn't been wrong. I had teared up several times looking at that picture.

When Jaxon finally tore his gaze from the picture, he looked right at me like he had just solved a puzzle. "Wait, my mom's having a baby."

"Yeah," I replied skeptically. I recognized that tone in his voice.

"And you're her husband."

"Uh huh."

"That means, you . . . you guys . . . ugh!" his face scrunched up in a disgusted expression. "That means you guys did it! Yuck! How could you do that? That's disgusting! Where's my barf tray?"

Addison dropped her face in her hands, trying not to laugh. I didn't even bother trying. I threw my head back and belly laughed harder than I had in a while.

"How do you even know about that?" I asked when he finally stopped ranting about how disgusting we were and how he was never, ever doing *that*. "You're only nine. We haven't had that conversation yet."

"My other dad told me," he answered. "When Shawn's

mom had a baby. I asked him how it got in her tummy and he told me."

"When you were *five*?" Addison asked, sitting straight up on the bed. Apparently this was news to her.

"What?" Jaxon shrugged. "I asked."

Thank you for that, Austin. That's one less difficult conversation I have to have.

She just shook her head, trying really hard not to find the humor in the whole situation.

"But I didn't know that *you* did that!" he said, still looking disgusted. "How could you do something so gross?"

"Well, someday you'll understand, and I don't think now is the time to explain it," I said calmly. "How about this—just pretend your mom ate some magical baby-making seed and it planted in her belly. Then you don't have to think about it."

"Ugh. I'll try," Jaxon said, picking up his Legos again. His nose was still scrunched like he had smelled something foul. "Because just thinking about it makes me want to throw up more than when I had that chemo."

Addison and I both started laughing again, partly because it *was* funny, but mostly because his reaction—his witty, snarky reaction—was a huge sign that he was finally on the mend. And in that moment, we both knew it.

Chapter FOURTEEN

"So, Jason," Judy began, "Adam tells me you want to start a foundation that promotes finding and keeping bone marrow donors."

"Sure do," I said as I sat in Judy's office. I had come up with the idea on my way home the day we found out about the baby, and I'd called Adam as soon as I could. He had thought the idea was a great one and immediately set up a meeting with Judy so we could go over legalities and crap like that. I didn't care what they had to do behind the scenes. I just knew I'd finally found something I could gladly put my name behind. "After no one in our family came up as a match for Jax, I started doing some research about it. I kept running into stories like ours and how common that was. And how there was a huge need for specific kinds of donors."

"What kinds of specific donors?" she asked.

"In a nutshell? Anyone with a diverse ethnic background."

Her eyebrows rose slightly. "Sounds like you've done

some research. Explain."

I smiled, appreciating how no-nonsense she always was at these meetings. "When I came up with the idea, I started looking at the bone marrow registry websites. One of the things I kept running into is how they need ethnically diverse donors."

"Why?" she asked, sitting back in her chair.

"As more and more people are born who are of mixed race, the need for mixed race donors has gone up," I said, my thoughts running a mile a minute. "I realized that football is one of the most ethnically diverse sports out there. I have black teammates and white teammates and Hispanic teammates. I've even had a couple Native Hawaiian teammates, and Hawaii is a tiny little state." I looked over at Adam. "You remember Robert Stoker? I used to play with him in college. He plays for Arizona now, I think."

"Yeah," Adam said, nodding. "Real nice guy."

"He is. Well, his dad was this huge Irish dude. Navy man. Met Robert's mom in the Philippines. Married her and brought her back to the states," I explained. "So Robert and all his siblings—and there are a bunch—are half Irish, half Filipino. I don't know for sure, but I'm guessing his bone marrow type might be pretty specific."

Judy stayed silent. I could practically see the gears turning in her brain.

"My point is," I said, "with thousands of ethnically diverse players, that means millions of ethnically diverse fans. If just one percent of those fans became bone marrow donors, there's no telling how many children's lives could be saved. Not just children, but adults too," I tacked on quickly.

I sat back, done talking. Now I just had to wait to see what Judy thought. She finally leaned forward and put her arms on her desk, leaning in toward the conversation.

"You know part of my job is to make sure that anything our players get involved with casts the organization in a good light." I nodded as she continued. "I knew this was a great idea when Adam told me about it, but seeing your passion and the research you've put in confirms it. Consider the organization in one hundred percent support of your new foundation."

I smiled. "Thanks, Judy. But, you know I'd be doing it with or without your support, right?"

She chuckled. "I know, Jason. It just makes it easier on you if we're behind you when you do. Also, because I think it's a great idea on a personal level, I've decided to help you guys get this launched on sort of a volunteer basis until it gets up and running."

"Really?" I asked. I hadn't been expecting that. Judy was a busy woman and one of the best in her field. To get her help was going to open up doors we didn't even know were coming yet.

"Sure am," she confirmed, reaching in her drawer for some paper. "In fact, I was sort of goofing around with some ideas last night, and I may have come up with an idea for a name and logo."

She slid the paper across the desk toward me. I looked down.

"Judy," I breathed. "This is great. You sure you don't mind if we use this as the name and logo? I feel like we're doing you an injustice by not paying you for this idea."

"Oh, don't you worry about that," she said, reaching into her drawer again. "Not only will I be taking credit for that when anyone asks where it came from, it's going into my resume portfolio. You never know when you're gonna need it."

"Absolutely," I chuckled. "Can I ask why you chose these colors?"

"Sure," she said with a smile. "You know the ribbons people wear in support of different causes?" I nodded. "That gold is the color for childhood cancer. The purple is for all cancers, not just ones that affect children."

My eyes widened. "You just thought of everything, didn't you?"

"There's more," Adam said. "Judy and I already talked about an idea for an event we want to run by you."

I looked at him with my eyes narrowed. "If this *event* is a black tie affair, count me out."

"Dude, I've worked with you for years," he said. "The last thing I want to do is hear you bitching about having to wear a tux. Give me a little credit."

"Okay, fine," I said, relaxing back into my chair. "So tell me about this event."

"We're going to do a bone marrow drive here at the stadium," she said, flipping through her notebook and looking through her notes. The idea officially had my attention. "Obviously I'm going to have to get approval before we set everything in stone. But the idea is that the bone marrow registry team sets up shop in the stadium to take applications, do the bone marrow interviews, draw blood or do cheek swaps, all the things they need to do to get someone signed up for the registry. Once the donor has completed that process, they get to spend ten minutes on the field."

"We're going to ask all the players and coaches to volunteer a couple hours of their time to be on the field talking to people and taking pictures," Adam chimed in. "It could be a real team event."

"You think they would go for that?" I asked. "I haven't had time to really talk to anyone about all this because I've been coming home during my off days. But do you think they'd do it?"

"Jay, I don't think you realize how many times these guys have approached me asking what they can do to help," Adam answered seriously. "This will be the first time they can make a difference in something that could directly affect Jaxon. You never know when one of these new donors will be his match."

"Not to mention, it would be great PR for the team," Judy added. "The better the PR for the team, the more people are moved by the effort. The more people are moved—"

"The more they register," I interrupted.

"Exactly," she said with a smile.

I shook my head with a smile on my face, overwhelmed by this idea and by how many people were willing to help out with it. "I'm going to let you guys sort out all the details. Just let me know where I need to be and when. And Adam, I trust you. If we need to hire people to run Hart to Heart," I said, looking at Judy, who smiled when I used the name. "Then do it. Just keep me in the loop."

"I will keep you updated every step of the way," he assured me. "I know we'll have to hire people at some point, but hopefully we can at least pull off this one event before we need to look into that."

I nodded and took a deep breath, just absorbing how fast

this was all moving. Hart to Heart was happening. And with any luck, it was going to help save some lives.

Chapter FIFTEEN

"What the fuck are we watching?" Deuce whispered to me as we stood in the back of the hospital great room, watching the kids' version of "entertainment." Now that the regular season had started and we were back home, I had convinced Deuce to come to the hospital to meet the kids and talk football with them. But first we had to get through this part.

"It's a puppet show, Deuce," I answered quietly. "You've never taken Trace to a puppet show before?"

"No, because I don't want my son growing up to be a pansy, but I know enough about them to know you're not supposed to be able to see the person with his hand up the puppet's ass," he whispered again. "That's just asking for some little kid to have nightmares about turning and coughing."

I snickered.

"And someone really needs to tell him his hot dog stand is open for business," Deuce added. "This is the children's ward. It's about to get real inappropriate, real quick."

I heard someone laugh next to Deuce and looked over to see a kid, probably around fifteen or sixteen, in a wheelchair and missing a leg. He glanced up at me when he saw me looking at him.

"Sorry, man," he said. "I wasn't trying to eavesdrop. But I was just thinking that his fly is down for all the world to see."

Deuce immediately pushed away from the wall now that he knew he was the center of someone's attention. "Deuce Johnson," Deuce said, putting out his hand to the kid.

"I know who you are," he said, shaking Deuce's hand. "Alex LeBaron."

"You a football fan, man?"

"Pfft. I'm not just a fan, man," the kid shot back. "I was one of the best tight ends in the state until this happened," he said, gesturing toward his missing leg.

"What happened, anyway?"

"Osteosarcoma. They had to cut off my leg to keep it from spreading," he said nonchalantly. "Hopefully I'll get my prosthesis in the next couple months now that my treatment is almost over."

"That sucks."

"Hell of a lot better than dying," the kid answered. "Plus, I have learned that the ladies are really into cripples like me. I plan on getting some hotties on my lap as soon as I get back to school."

I snickered again.

"What? I'm just giving them a ride to class," he defended. "Consider it like a taxi service."

Oh yeah. Deuce had met his match.

"You guys ready for the season? Seems like you ran into a little trouble on your offensive line last year. Did you get that fixed?" Alex asked.

I laughed as I continued to watch the exchange. Nothing riled Deuce up like someone questioning the inner workings of the team.

"Man, we're gonna have no problems this year," Deuce bragged. "We've been working on our passing game and have some great plays that you've never even dreamed up before!"

"Uh huh," Alex said skeptically. "I heard you say that during the pre-season interviews last year, too. Didn't happen."

"What?" Deuce asked. "What the hell are you talking about? We got rid of Thompson and have Duchess this year. You can't be more prepared than that!"

"Dude, I may not be able to play anymore, but I've still got eyes," Alex bantered back. "Those two might as well be the same person with the way they play."

I chuckled and redirected my attention back to the puppet show, which was finally wrapping up. Deuce wouldn't need any of my attention for a while.

"Hey, Jason!" Jax yelled, launching himself into my arms. "Where's my mom?"

"She went to go fill out a bunch of paperwork since you're getting out today. Are you excited?"

"Yeah," he said, with a little less enthusiasm than normal. I thought for sure not having to do any more chemo would make him really excited.

"You don't sound all that thrilled, little man. What's up?"

He looked down and spoke softly. "I'm just gonna miss my friends. I know I have friends at school, but I get to see them every day. I won't see my new friends unless I come back."

I put him down and squatted down next to him. "Buddy, you can see your friends anytime you'd like. Your mom and I made some friends while we were here too. We all have friends we're gonna keep up with, okay?"

He nodded as we walked out of the room, leaving Deuce to his new friend. "Did you enjoy the puppet show?" I asked as I rubbed his bald head. After his meds were changed, all his hair had gone ahead and fallen out. In true Jaxon fashion, he didn't seem to notice, or even care.

"I don't know," he answered seriously. "I couldn't stop looking at his zipper being open."

I barked a laughed as we made our way into his room where Addison waited for us.

"Hey, little man," she said with a smile on her face. "Are you ready to go home?"

"Do I have to go back to school?" he asked as he climbed onto the bed, reaching for his Nintendo DS.

"Let's wait and see what the doctor says," she answered with a roll of her eyes. "He's gonna do one last check-in with us here in a few minutes."

Right on cue, Dr. Bates walked in the door. "Jaxon!" he said with a big smile on his face. "How's one of my favorite patients doing?"

"Good," he answered without looking up from his game.

"He's a little sad about leaving his friends," I answered. "And apparently he doesn't want to go back to school."

"Ah," the doctor said with understanding. "Well, let's look you over real quick and I'll let you know if you're school-ready before you go."

While they did a quick once-over, Addison and I finished packing up. It was amazing how much crap one tiny hospital room could accumulate in six weeks' time. And we had stayed the entire six weeks. Since it took some time to find the meds that didn't make Jax so sick and that actually worked for him, it extended our stay.

"Well," Dr. Bates finally said, "I'd say you look almost as healthy as a horse."

"That's great news," Addison said with relief. "So we're still good to leave today?"

"Oh yeah, without a doubt."

"Do I have to go back to school yet?" Jax asked.

"I think you probably need to keep with a tutor for a few more weeks, just to make sure you're fully up to speed," he answered. "But I'll see you in about a month and we can discuss the issue of school then, okay?"

"Okay!" Jaxon said excitedly.

"What about going out in public?" I asked. "The season started last month. You think he can go to a game? Or is that too much on his immune system?"

"I wouldn't take him out every single day, but taking him to a game every once in a while should be fine. *As long as he feels up to it*," he emphasized. "Remember, his body is still working on recovering. We don't want to push him too hard."

I looked over at Jaxon, who was beaming. Going to my games was one of his very favorite things, so this was a real boost for him and me both.

"So I will see you guys in about a month for your follow-up, okay?" the doctor asked, rising from his chair.

"Thank you, Dr. Bates," Addison said, giving him a quick hug. "Thank you for everything."

"It has truly been my pleasure, Addison," he answered with a smile. As he headed out the door, Bri walked in.

"Hey! How's my squirt-gun buddy doing?" she asked with a big smile. "Are you ready to go home?"

"Yep!" Jaxon said. "Are you gonna come visit me?"

"Don't you worry about that," she said. "I'm sure we'll

see each other around."

"Bri, we really can't thank you enough for taking such good care of him," I said as I zipped up the last of the suitcases. "I know you made it so much more fun than it could have been."

"Well, he's a special boy," she said smiling fondly at him. "Anyway, I know you're heading out, but I just wanted to make sure you guys still have my cell phone number."

I pulled out my phone and searched through my contacts until I found it. "Yep, right here. I'm hoping I never have to use it."

She chuckled. "Yeah, if I never hear from you again, that will be fine by me."

Addison approached her and gave her a quick hug as well. "I agree. As much fun as you have been, I hope we never see you again," she joked.

"Agreed," Bri said, giving Jax a big hug. "Anyway, I'm headed back to work, but you guys take care of yourselves."

"Bye, Bri," Jaxon said as she walked out the door.

"So," I said, clapping my hands and rubbing them together. "Now that we're ready to blow this joint, do we need to make any stops on the way home?"

"Yes!" Jaxon said excitedly. "For pancakes!"

"Pancakes it is!" I responded as we grabbed our bags and left the hospital room, hopeful that we would never see the inside of it again.

We finally had Jaxon settled in bed for the night, and the house was quiet. The whole family was excited about his homecoming and had invaded our house, bringing signs and balloons and food. It turned into a regular late-night party. But that was no surprise.

I sat down on the couch next to Addison, who was relaxing with her feet up, rubbing her expanding baby pooch.

"How are you feeling?" I asked, propping my feet up next to hers.

"I feel like I can finally breathe again," she said, looking over at me with a relaxed smile on her face.

"It is nice to be home," I said, leaning my face toward hers so our foreheads were touching.

"I am so looking forward to sleeping in a real bed for more than just a few hours. I feel like I haven't slept in six weeks."

"You haven't," I replied, brushing some hair off her forehead. "You know what else we haven't done in six weeks."

She giggled. "I'm sorry, Jason. For a newlywed, you are sorely lacking in the sex department."

"Eh," I said, waving her off. "Between you spending the night at the hospital, me being gone, and getting all the foundation stuff started, it's not like we were ignoring each other. We just had to let life run its course for a while."

"You're too good to us, you know that?"

"I'm hoping you'll make it up to me tonight," I answered, waggling my eyebrows.

Addison smiled before standing up and grabbing my hand. "Come on. We have some catching up to do." She dragged me down the hall to our bedroom. Although, I didn't really have to be coerced or anything. I was definitely a willing participant.

As soon as the bedroom door was closed, I couldn't keep myself off her anymore. I hadn't kissed her that deeply in weeks, and I was immediately ready to rip our clothes off and go to town. She didn't seem to mind.

Within seconds, we were on the bed, stark naked. I finally tore myself away from her mouth and took a moment to peruse my wife's body. It had been too long since I had seen it. I hadn't even realized how much her body had changed because of the pregnancy. I reached down to cup her breasts and found they were much more solid and felt full. When I pinched her nipple, she flinched.

"Ow," she gasped, pushing my hand away. "Don't pinch. They're really sore right now."

"Really?" I asked. "I didn't know that happened. Do they feel, I don't know, heavy to you?"

"Kind of," she answered. "They just feel kind of swollen. And they're definitely more sensitive. I swear now that they're so sore I keep whacking them on stuff."

I smiled as I ran my hand down her rib cage, making my way to her stomach. Sure enough, what was usually a soft pooch was more rounded and solid. And her hips were just slightly more wide than normal. Not a lot, but it made her curvier.

"My god, you are so beautiful," I breathed as I kissed my way down to her stomach. "Can you feel anything in here yet?" I asked as I kissed her belly and rubbed my hands over it. The thought that my baby was in there just blew my mind.

"Oh yeah. She moves around all the time," she said.

"Really?" I asked, looking up into her eyes, intrigued by every single thing she had to tell me. We hadn't had any time to have these simple conversations until now, so it was all brand new. "You can feel him this early?"

She put her hands behind her head, propping herself up, and smirked down at me. "Or her," she corrected me.

It was a good-natured argument we continued to have. I was convinced this baby was a boy. I don't think Addison cared either way. But she liked ribbing me about having a daughter.

"It's not necessarily normal to feel it at fourteen weeks, but look who her daddy is," she chuckled. "She is very active, and I'm sure she's huge."

I kissed her stomach one more time before making my way back up to her mouth. "I can't believe I'm admitting this to you, but I really am kind of worried about hurting *him* during sex."

Addison smiled up at me. "Baby, I promise you won't hurt *her*," she said, rubbing her hands over the scruff on my face. "She's padded up nice and secure in there. There's no way you're getting in. And no, you won't be able to impale her, so don't even go there."

"I'm going to assume that's not an insult to my manhood," I said with mock offense.

She giggled. "Oh, your manhood is just fine. Except it's not in me yet, so I need you to stop worrying and make love to me already."

She didn't have to ask me twice. As she wrapped her legs around me, I pushed inside of her, and we both groaned with relief. It had been way too long. Now that things were settling down, I was determined not to put our sex life on the backburner again. We needed to feel connected to each other, and she still needed some reassurance that I found her to be the sexiest woman alive.

As I devoured her mouth again, I brought both her hands above her head and pinned them there with one of mine. I loved her in this position. I loved watching the way her body stretched out in front of me and how open it was to my touch. I felt like I could reach anywhere on her in this position, and it brought out the primal urges in me.

As I continued to plunge in and out of her, her breathing accelerated. That was one nice surprise I learned about her long ago . . . She didn't need me to manipulate her body in any special way to have an orgasm. Just being inside her could bring her intense pleasure. Made my job more fun.

I leaned down to flick her sensitive nipple with my tongue, and she broke apart underneath me. I followed right behind her with a deep groan.

As we caught our breath, I continued showering her neck and chest with kisses. Damn, I had missed this.

"Damn, I missed that," she said, echoing my thoughts exactly. I chuckled as I kissed her one last time and pulled out of her with a hiss.

"Stay right here. I'll get a washcloth."

"No can do, big man," she said, reaching for my hand so I could pull her up. "It's not just my boobs and stomach that are changing. I have to pee all the time. I won't make it through the night if I don't go again."

I held her hand, leading her toward the bathroom to get cleaned up. "I guess that means sneezing is out of the question."

She snorted as we parted ways—her to the toilet, me to the washcloths. "Don't even joke about that. I actually peed on myself the other day when I sneezed."

I barked a laugh. "Are you serious?"

"Welcome to the wonderful and sexy world of pregnancy, babe," she said through the door. "Just wait until my last trimester when I randomly fart. I'm gonna be really sexy then."

I leaned against the doorjamb as she finished up. "This could be a very entertaining few months for the men around this house."

"I'm sure you and Jaxon will have a great time making fun of me."

"Oh no. We'll just join you," I said with a smile as I dragged her back to bed. "If you get to fart whenever you feel the need, so do we."

She chuckled and stifled a yawn as we settled into bed, her tucked in my arms. "Looking forward to it," she said sarcastically before I felt her fall asleep.

Chapter SIXTEEN

I ran through the tunnel of the stadium amidst the cheers of the crowd. My eyes scanned the stands, looking for Addison and Jaxon. As soon as I found them, I smacked my helmet twice and pointed at them. They both pointed back. Somehow that one gesture turned into a tradition, and I did it at every single game they came to.

I knew I needed to keep my focus on the game ahead, but I was just so excited to have my family back together and cheering me on, I couldn't help the goofy grin on my face. It's amazing how good regular everyday things feel when you've been dragged through some of the hardest times of your life.

As we all tossed the ball around and went through our pre-game routines, I heard my own voice come through all the speakers in the stadium. I looked up and saw the public service announcement we had filmed a couple of weeks ago for Hart to Heart being aired on all the Jumbotrons in the room. My teammates all noticed too.

It was the first time the PSA had run, which meant it was

simultaneously being aired on national television as well. I couldn't help but shoot up a small prayer that people would respond to it and look for more information on how to get involved. Jaxon may have been out of the woods for now, but there were thousands of kids out there who were still fighting for their lives. Any one of them could find their match through this program.

As soon as the PSA was over, Jax's shiny bald head popped up on the screen. I knew the announcers were talking about him now, but Jax didn't seem to mind. As soon as Addison pointed him out on the screen, he immediately began waving to the fans. The crowd roared in response, and I watched as people gave him a standing ovation. I felt more pride at that moment than I had during all of my previous games combined.

All I did was play football. But my kid had fought for his life and won. The feeling was overwhelming.

"He is quite the little show-off, isn't he?" Deuce asked as he walked up to me, patting me on the back.

"He's been hanging out with you too much," I responded with a smile.

"Oh no, don't blame me," Deuce argued. "That kid came with his own ego."

I snickered. Yeah. Deuce was right. But I would never admit to it.

Three hours later, we all barreled into the locker room. We had beaten the Saints 21 – 14, so we were all amped up, high fiving each other and hooting and hollering. Normal post-victory celebrations.

"All right, I need everyone to fall in, please, fall in!" we heard Coach Ramiro yell. He waited a few more minutes for everyone to calm down before he started talking.

"First of all, that was a great game tonight. You did your

jobs and did it well. We still need to work on conditioning, so be ready for some drills on Monday." A murmur went through the room, as we all knew "some drills" meant we'd be sore that night.

"Okay, quiet down, quiet down. I have some news," Coach said. I sat down on the bench and started unwrapping the tape off my wrists. "You all saw Jason's PSA before the game about his new foundation. I don't know how much you guys have heard about it, but the goal is to get more bone marrow donors to sign up for the bone marrow registry. Jaxon never found a match. Fortunately, he doesn't seem to need one right now, since he's on the mend."

The team responded with clapping and cheers and a few pats on my back in congratulations. When they quieted down, Coach continued. "We're having an event here at the stadium in about a month, and I'm asking for you all to seriously consider donating at least a couple hours of your time to meet these fans. The more players who are going to be here, the more people we'll get to sign up, and that's the goal. Keep in mind, this is on a voluntary basis. I'm not paying you to be here, so don't be a douche and expect to be compensated. This is about saving lives people, not feeding your egos." A few chuckles echoed through the room. "Also, I got a phone call this morning from Dan Ryley. He's an assistant coach in Denver. Some of you may know him. Apparently he lost his little girl about fifteen years ago to the same kind of cancer Jaxon had." I leaned forward, resting my elbows on my knees, not sure where he was going with this. I had met Dan several times but had no idea he had lost a child to leukemia.

"Anyway, Dan heard about the event we have coming up and liked the idea so much he's convinced the Denver Broncos to have the same kind of event in conjunction with ours. People registering, people touring their field, the whole bit."

I felt a huge smile cross my face. I knew the event was a good idea when Adam had pitched it to me, but to know another team had picked up on it and was piggybacking on the idea to reach more people . . . I never expected that.

"During the call, Dan patched in the NFL commissioner."

Any remaining sounds stopped at that statement. It's like the entire room froze.

"The commissioner is thrilled about this idea. Says it's exactly the kind of thing we all need to be involved with. So he is encouraging every single team in the NFL to participate in this bone marrow drive. He's getting with Judy first thing tomorrow to go over the plans she has so they can be implemented at the other stadiums. Congratulations, Jason," he said, turning to me. "Looks like Hart to Heart is going nationwide."

My head fell into my hands as the tears started to fall, teammates clapping me on the back and shouting congratulations in my direction. Never in my wildest dreams did I think this could happen. This little foundation that started to help Jaxon find a bone marrow donor, one he might not even need now, would help saves dozens, maybe even hundreds of lives.

I finally pulled myself together enough to stand up, a smile on my face. "Thank you, Coach," I said, grabbing him in a bear hug. "This is such great news. I can't wait to tell my family."

"It's all you, Jay," he responded. "You did all the hard work. Now hit the showers. You have a press conference to be at in five minutes. And when they ask about Hart to Heart, tell them more teams are planning to join us. Let's get the word out there."

"Yes, sir," I said, heading for the showers. I couldn't wait to give this announcement. Hart to Heart was already a success.

Hart to Heart day arrived a month later. Between practices, games, doctor's appointments for both Jaxon and Addison, and getting everything set up for the bone marrow drive, it had been a long few weeks. It was a nicer exhaustion than the kind I felt when Jaxon was in the hospital, though. This exhaustion felt productive.

I walked around the four "corners" of the stadium, where the donor booths were set up. Each area had several desks set up behind portable partitions. It was where the potential donors would come to fill out paperwork, answer questions, and get their blood drawn.

I made my way around to the tunnel where the field tours would start. After a few brainstorming sessions, we decided to use some staff members as makeshift tour guides. It streamlined the whole thing and gave us some people to be the point of contact in case anyone had any questions.

Tours would go in groups of twenty or thirty, up to four tours at a time. They would all get fifteen minutes on the field to take pictures, talk with players or just sit on the bench and take it all in.

My teammates had really stepped up, too. Almost everyone had signed up for at least an hour of hobnobbing. Most for two hours or more. I felt really confident that the fans were going to be pleased with their tours.

As I walked through the tunnel and onto the field, I

looked up to see a giant banner with a picture of Jaxon and me on it. He had his happiest smile on, despite his bald head. I had a more somber look on my face. It was still a great picture of us, though. The logo Judy had come up with was in the upper right-hand corner, and the caption at the bottom read, "Because *you* can save a life."

I was really proud of Jaxon for being willing to be the poster boy for the foundation. Not a lot of kids would be okay with having a giant picture of them taken after six weeks of chemo and blasted around the country for everyone to see.

"Well?" Judy asked as she walked toward me with a clipboard in hand. "What do you think?"

I dug my hands into my front pockets. "It's amazing, Judy. Everything looks great. How many people do we have signed up?"

She looked down at her clipboard, sorting through until she found what she was looking for. "At last count we had roughly twenty-five hundred people scheduled. I'm sure we'll have a few extras, though."

"What about the other stadiums? Do you know?"

"They're all running about the same. Twenty-five hundred people times thirty-one stadiums . . . That's almost seventy-eight *thousand* new potential bone marrow matches in four hours' time."

"Holy shit," I breathed. "That's incredible, Judy. I can't thank you enough for helping us get this done."

"Eh, don't thank me," she said dismissively. "You know half these people wouldn't even be here if it weren't for the promise of a field tour. Oh! How is Jaxon, anyway? Didn't he have his follow-up appointment the other day?"

"Sure did," I said with a smile. "So far, his counts look good. He's not back to one hundred percent yet, and we'll still have check-ups every few months for a while, but he's still in remission."

"That's wonderful! I'm so glad for you guys!" she exclaimed as she looked down at her watch. "Oh shoot. I need to head out and make sure security is ready to go. We'll be opening the doors in about thirty minutes."

"Sounds good. Thanks again," I said with a wave as she walked away.

As I turned, I heard another voice behind me.

"Hey, Hart!" Adam yelled. "Look what I found hiding at the airport."

I turned around, and my mouth dropped open.

"What are you doing here?" I asked as Sara came in for a big hug.

"Are you kidding? I wasn't going to miss this!" she said. "Anything I can do to help my fake boyfriend's kid, ya know."

I laughed. Sara had spent years using me as her "date" whenever we were in the same city. I knew she was gay and dating her manager, Elaine, but for personal reasons, she wasn't ready to come out to the world yet. It didn't matter to me. I treasured her friendship and was excited she had surprised me like this.

"Where's Elaine?" I asked. "Did she come with you?"

"She's up in Judy's office, fielding some media calls," she said. "What do you need me to do? Are there any particular jobs that need to be filled, or do you want me to meet fans? You tell me. I'm here for the whole day."

"I honestly don't know," I said with a shrug. "Adam and Judy have really coordinated everything with all the volunteers. What do you think, Adam?"

"I think it would just be great if you signed autographs and hung out with all the fans," he said, twirling his keys around his finger. "Everyone coming knows to expect football players, but it'll be a nice surprise to have a Hollywood face, too."

"I can do that," she smiled. "Whatever you guys need."

"What I need is for you to say you and Elaine will come over for dinner tonight. I know Addison will be excited you're here. Do you need a place to stay? We've got plenty of room."

"We're already staying at the Marriott by the airport since we leave early tomorrow morning. But we'll take you up on that offer of dinner."

"Great!"

"Don't forget to text Addison and let her know," she said as she and Adam started to walk away to get her all set up. "You know she'll be mad if you spring this on her last minute and she doesn't have enough food!"

"I'll let her know right now," I said as I pulled my phone out of my pocket.

"Smart man!" she yelled and took off across the field, catching up with Adam, who wasn't slowing down to wait for her. I chuckled. He was such a putz sometimes.

Me: You will never guess who came into town to help out.

Addison: If I'll never guess, just go ahead and tell me. You know I hate this game.

Me: Sara and Elaine

Addison: Really?? Invite them over for dinner! I'm making fish!

Me: Ew. What kind.

Addison: The good kind that you like. INVITE THEM TO DINNER!

Me: The kind I get to grill? Awesome. Already invited them. Just giving you a heads up.

Addison: Tell Sara I said thanks for reminding you to tell me.

Me: LOL. Will do. Love you, babe.
Addison: Love you, too.

Two hours later, things were in full swing. New donors were being added to the database. Tours were controlled chaos. And everyone seemed happy.

I talked with people and took lots of pictures. Was given a lot of well wishes and heard stories of children with cancer that sounded so similar to ours. It was intense. More emotionally intense than I realized it would be. But the adrenaline of what was happening canceled out any exhaustion I might have felt.

I turned to introduce myself to the next people in line, but I recognized the face immediately.

"Hey Jason," he said, shaking my hand. "You probably don't remember me. We met in the hospital a couple months ago. I'm . . ."

"Roger," I said, interrupting him. "Yeah, man, of course I remember you. How've you been?"

"Good, good," he said, turning to the woman standing next to him. "This is my wife, Joy."

"It's nice to meet you," I said, shaking her hand as well. "How's Iris, anyway? Is she hanging on?"

They looked at each other before Roger spoke up. "She passed away a few days after we last spoke. She just couldn't fight it anymore."

I wasn't sure quite how to describe the feelings coursing through me. I was shocked because the whole time we were in the hospital, I hadn't seen a child die. I'd seen a lot get close, but never actually met anyone who lost their child.

And I was overwhelmingly sad for Roger and Joy. My heart literally ached. That could have been us. That could have been Jaxon. I was so happy that it hadn't been Jaxon.

That, of course, made me feel guilty that it was them and not me. And I felt all of it in less than half a second's time.

"Oh god, man," I breathed. "I don't even know what to say."

He shrugged. "There's nothing to say. It sucks." I could see the tears welling up in both their eyes as they remembered their little girl. "She put up a good fight though. Our girl was a warrior with that brain tumor."

"Yeah, she was," I agreed. I had never met Iris. Hadn't even seen her. But for her to fight that tumor as long as she had at such a young age . . . Warrior was the right word.

"What are you guys doing here, anyway? Did you sign up for the registry?"

"Sure did," he said with a smile. "We saw the commercial on TV about this and realized, during the entire time we were dealing with Iris's illness, we never signed up for the registry. Can you believe that?"

I smiled. "Well, you were a little busy."

"True. But now, well, we know there's nothing anyone can do for Iris anymore," Joy said, speaking up for the first time in the conversation. "But we can't ever let another parent go through what we did if we can help it."

"I just . . . god, you guys . . ." I stumbled. "That's just about one of the most selfless things I've heard today."

Joy shrugged.

"It's just the right thing to do," Roger said.

I nodded as we heard the buzz, indicating that round of tours was over and it was time to clear the field.

"Hey, do you mind if we take a picture that I can post on my Facebook page?" I asked them before they could walk away.

"Sure," they both said, shrugging.

We took a quick selfie and said our goodbyes. As they walked off the field, I quickly uploaded the picture with the caption, "Lost their daughter and still working to help other kids with cancer. These are MY heroes. #neverforgetiris. #harttoheart."

Not only did they show me what it was to truly keep their priorities straight, even after the worst had already happened, but they sparked another idea for the foundation that would hopefully help a lot of other families.

I quickly texted Adam with the basics of the idea. If anyone could get it to work, it would be him.

Then I got ready for another round of fans to come through that tunnel, with a big smile on my face.

Chapter SEVENTEEN

It was one of those rare moments when Addison and I were alone. Jaxon was with Mick, shopping for fishing poles or something. So it was just the two of us.

Alone in the house.

For hours.

So of course we were making out on the couch like a couple of teenagers.

I wish I could take credit for our recent rash of love making, but it was all Addison. She was twenty weeks pregnant and those second-trimester hormones were making her horny.

All the time.

Not that I was complaining. There was nothing in the world I enjoyed more than being inside her. So how we ended up on the couch, engaging in heavy petting while fully clothed, was beyond me.

"What time is Jax coming home?" I asked as I went to the hem of her shirt, determined to finally get down to the good stuff.

"He's spending the night at Mick's house," she said, beating me to it and ripping her shirt over her head.

I grunted in approval as I looked down at her breasts. Her white lacy bra was barely containing them anymore, and it made the brain in my pants very, very happy. "Good, because I don't think I can make it to the bedroom. I'm gonna take you right here on this couch."

She giggled and then gasped when I gently bit her nipple through the lace. "I'm getting kind of fat, babe. I think you'd better bend me over the couch if we're gonna do it in here."

I'm pretty sure I almost lost my load just by those words alone. "Get these pants off. Now," I growled.

We made quick work of her pants, and I kissed my way down her body to the juncture of her thighs before she spoke again. "Jason," she breathed. "You have too many clothes on and I have to pee."

And that screeched my assault on her body to a sudden halt. "You didn't just ruin the mood, did you? We have no child in the house, and you just ruined the mood."

"Oh no I didn't," she said, climbing out from under me and leaning over seductively to kiss me again. "Because while I'm gone, I want you to get naked. And when I get back, you'd better be sitting right there stroking yourself slowly, up and down . . . up . . . and . . . down . . . making yourself nice and ready for me." Then she did the last thing I expected. She dropped her bra on my lap, dragged her nipples across my face before I could react, and walked away, hips swaying as she laughed.

Holy.

Fuck.

Did that woman know how to tease me. She had so much more confidence in the bedroom than she did when we had been dating. Something about being married built up that last little bit of trust that she needed to let her confidence in her own sex appeal finally show.

Or, she was just in her second trimester and horny as hell. Either way, I got naked faster than I ever had in my life. When she came out from the bathroom, I was doing exactly what she asked . . . sitting naked on the furniture, stroking myself, thinking about all the ways I was going to take her during our night off from parenthood.

She, on the other hand, was wearing yoga pants and a sweatshirt. Not exactly what I was anticipating to see while I whacked in the main room.

"Um, so I wasn't planning on killing the mood," she started.

"But . . ."

"But we probably need to call the doctor real fast."

"Why?" I asked as my hand finally stopped its up and down movements.

"Wellllll, I'm sort of bleeding."

"Meaning what?"

"Meaning you're not supposed to bleed during pregnancy, and we probably need to go get it checked out before continuing with our romp around the room."

I sighed as I reached for my boxer briefs, and she reached for the phone.

"I'm sorry, babe," she said as she dialed. "I was looking forward to christening the couch as much as you were."

"I know," I said, kissing her on top of the head and buttoning my pants. "Sex can wait. Take care of baby first."

Ten minutes later, we were dressed and on the road, headed to see the doctor who said to just come on in.

"Are you having any pain?" I asked her. Now that my

brain wasn't as sex scrambled, I started to realize that this wasn't a good situation. But she was so nonchalant about it, I wasn't really sure if I should be worried.

"Mmm . . . a little. But it's more like my uterus is stretching or something. Or maybe it's my muscles. I don't really know," she said dismissively.

"You don't really seem worried about this."

"It's not that I'm not worried. It's just, well, there's not a lot we can do until we find out what's happening. I'm trying not to make a big deal out of it yet."

That made me feel a little better. "I can't believe I just got cock blocked by this kid before he's even born."

She laughed. "*She's* been hanging around with Jaxon too much."

I snorted. "Ain't that the truth." The little stinker still didn't have the whole *Don't just barge into our room* rule mastered. Made it really hard to get wild and crazy in the bedroom when Addison had a thing about locking doors in case of emergency. There's just no logical parent lie to the question, "Why is your penis holding my naked mom up against the wall?" So I didn't want to go there.

We got to the waiting room of Dr. Plunkett's office and made ourselves comfortable on one of the big poufy couches. I wasn't sure why they were in an OB's office. There was no way a really pregnant woman would be able to maneuver herself back out of that couch.

I picked up one of the magazines while we waited. Not that there was much to choose from—Parenting, FitPregnancy, American Baby. I opted for the pamphlet about prenatal vitamins.

It wasn't a very intriguing read, so I started looking around. There were quite a few pregnant women sitting in the chairs scattered around the room. Just a couple of men, though. I guess it made sense, but I was kind of surprised by how many of the dads weren't there. I was so excited about this baby I couldn't stand it when I couldn't come to check ups.

I looked to my left and noticed some guy eyeing Addison. At least, I think he was eyeing Addison. Either way, I chose that moment to reach over and put my hand on her stomach. *Yeah . . . I did that. Look all you want, but that's* my *bump, asshole.*

"Why don't you just pee on my leg while you're at it," Addison said, not even looking up from the magazine she was flipping through, and quietly enough that I was the only one who heard.

"What are you talking about?"

"I'm talking about you staking your claim on me in front of that guy."

"Do you blame me?" I whispered. "He keeps checking you out."

"He's not checking me out, Jason. He has a lazy eye."

I turned my head to look at him again.

"Huh. Well, what do ya know," I said in acknowledgment. "He should get that looked at."

She snorted. "Yeah. You go right ahead and tell him he needs to go to the eye doctor. That'll look great in tomorrow's papers, Mr. Celebrity."

I shrugged as a nurse opened the door next to the receptionist desk.

"Addison?" she said with a smile. "You're up."

I popped up from the couch and watched as Addison struggled to get her body weight to shift forward so she could get up.

That's exactly why a poufy couch wasn't a good idea in

this office.

I reached down and grabbed her hands, helping her to her feet.

"Thanks," she said as she started walking toward the door.

"No, thank you," I replied. "You looked like a turtle on your back for a minute. It was the most entertaining part of this waiting room."

She rolled her eyes at me and smirked as we made our way to the back, following the nurse through all the regular triage stuff they did.

We were finally ushered into an exam room where Addison was handed a gown and instructed to take everything off and hop up on the table.

As I made myself comfortable, I looked around the room and spotted, what I assumed, was an ultrasound machine. But what caught my attention was the really long, wand-looking thing sticking up on the side.

"That is a really big fake-penis-looking thing," I said as Addison changed behind the curtain.

She snorted. "You're talking about the ultrasound machine, aren't you?"

"No. I'm talking about the big fake-penis-looking thing attached to the ultrasound machine."

"Jealous of a machine, Jason?" she teased as she came out from behind the curtain and climbed up on the table. "It is longer than you by at least a couple of inches."

"I got him on girth, baby," I said with a wink. "And skill."

She smacked her hand to her forehead as the door opened and Dr. Plunkett walked in.

"Hey, Addison," she said, heading to the sink to wash her

hands. "How's it going?"

"It was going fine until our little monster decided his daddy was having too much fun with our child-free day," I answered for her.

"Ohmygod," Addison said with exasperation. "Ignore him. He is in rare form today. I don't know what his deal is."

The doctor laughed. "I take it you have an ornery baby already, huh? Lie down for me."

"Jason seems to think so," Addison said as she lay back on the table. "But anything that gets in the way of his fun these days seems to be a tragedy in his eyes."

"Hmph," I grunted in response as the doctor pushed and prodded on Addison's stomach. "It depends on what kind of fun I'm trying to have."

"I take it you were in the middle of sex when you started bleeding?" the doctor asked as a nurse knocked and walked in the door.

"Nope," I said. "Got blocked before I even got that far."

"Like I said," Addison interrupted. "Ignore him."

"Okay, so no actual penetration before the bleeding started," the doctor clarified.

"No," Addison said, shaking her head as the nurse rolled the giant penis and its machine closer to the table. "I had to pee first. That's when I saw it."

"What color is the blood?"

"In between pink and red."

"Okay, let's see what's going on."

As the machine turned on, Dr. Plunkett squirted some goo on Addison's stomach and grabbed the *not* penis wand off the stand. "Sorry, man, looks like you got blocked too," I said to the machine under my breath. Addison smacked me on the chest.

As soon as the images started coming up on the monitor, the nurse turned the lights out, and we got a good look at our baby.

"Look at that good-looking kid," the doctor said. "Wow, you've got an active little baby, don't you?"

"Always," Addison said.

"Heartbeat looks nice and strong," she said, clicking a button on the machine. "Now that we've checked that, let's take a look at the placenta."

For the next several minutes, she moved the wand around, and we saw different parts of the baby and Addison's insides. Even I could see how active he was. His feet kept coming in and out of the picture, and one time it looked like he flipped off the camera. I thought it was funny. Addison just smacked me again.

"Oh . . . lookie there," the doctor said. "I'm pretty sure. . . yep . . . do you guys want to know the baby's sex?"

My mouth dropped open as I looked at Addison. "Really? You can see what it is?"

"Sure can," she said. "It's up to you guys if you want to know. Some people prefer to have the surprise in the delivery room."

"Do you want to know?" I asked Addison.

"Do you?"

"Hell yeah!" I replied with excitement.

"Then yes," Addison said. "Lay it on me, Dr. Plunkett. Am I still going to be outnumbered in my own home?"

"Sadly, yes," she replied with a smile. "It's a boy!"

"Ohmygod . . . it's a boy," I said, barely able to contain my excitement. "We're having a boy, Addison!"

She laughed as I tried not to jump out of the seat and fist pump the air.

"And he's okay?" I asked, suddenly feeling very protective of our little man. "There's nothing wrong with him?"

The nurse flipped the lights back on, as the doctor started putting things away.

"Everything looks great with him," she answered as she wiped Addison's bump clean of the gel stuff. "He looks healthy and he's measuring great. What I was most worried about was the placenta. But it's right where it's supposed to be. And your cervix looks nice and thick, too."

The nurse folded part of the table underneath Addison and helped her to a sitting position.

"So why am I bleeding?" Addison asked.

"That is the million dollar question," she said as she washed her hands again and sat back down in the rolling chair. "Everyone who has bleeding problems when they are pregnant wants an answer, but sometimes we just don't have one. Baby, placenta, and cervix look good. No pain. No cramping. It seems like perfectly normal pregnancy bleeding."

"So what do we do?"

"My recommendation: take it easy. When your body starts having strange, unexplained symptoms like these, it means you need a break. And your circumstances have been more stressful than the average person's lately."

"Yeah, but Jax is out of the hospital and doing great now," I said with a smile.

"Oh, that's great!" Dr. Plunkett said. "I'm glad to hear that. Last time you were here, he was still in treatment. I'm glad to see it worked."

"So are we," Addison agreed, squeezing my hand.

"That just makes it easier to take it easy," the doctor continued. "Stay off your feet while you're bleeding. Limit your activity. And listen to what your body is telling you."

"Wait, wait, wait . . ." I said, finally realizing a very important piece of this. "Are you saying no sex?"

Addison rolled her eyes, but the doctor just smiled.

"I'm saying I recommend you wait until she has been symptom-free for forty-eight hours before engaging in any form of penetration. And even then, being very careful not to get too rowdy."

"Buuuut, we can do other stuff right?"

"Okay," Addison interjected quickly. "Thank you, doctor, I think we get it."

"Anytime." She laughed while standing up and making her way out the door.

I couldn't believe it. I had just gotten sex back a few weeks before, and I was already being cut off again. But on the flip side . . .

We were having a boy.

That almost made up for the fact that he was a little cock blocker.

Almost.

Chapter EIGHTEEN

"**M**om?"

Through my sleep, I heard a soft voice. I couldn't figure out why I knew the voice. Maybe it was a dream.

"Mom," the voice said a little louder.

"Hmmm," I heard Addison say. That voice I recognized as I started pulling closer to consciousness.

"Mommy, I don't feel good," the voice said. It sounded like . . . Who was it? Jaxon. *Oh yeah*, I thought to myself. *Jaxon must be in our room for something.*

I felt Addison shuffle around and sit up as I got comfortable and started to fall back asleep. Then I heard her gasp.

"Jason, get up!" she said in the dark. I sat up slowly, rubbing my eyes, not quite sure what was happening or why she sounded so urgent.

"Jason, he's burning up," she said, launching herself out of bed as Jaxon climbed right in next to me. Next thing I knew, the lights were on and she was in the bathroom, rifling through cabinets and babbling something about a thermometer.

"What's wrong, buddy?" I asked as I reached over to stroke his head. He was burning up. "Holy shit, Addison. How high is his fever?"

"How should I know?" she retorted, moving the blankets around and the popping the thermometer under his arm since he had fallen back asleep. "I'm taking his temperature now."

We waited several minutes for his temperature to register. When the thermometer finally beeped and Addison took a look, she paled almost instantly. "Oh god. It's 102.7. Under his arm."

"What does that mean?" I asked.

"That means you add a degree. We have to take him to the hospital. Now."

In less than five minutes, we had managed to get dressed, brush our teeth, and gotten Jax in the back of my truck with a wet towel on his head, trying to get the fever down. He never woke up enough for us to get him to take any Children's Tylenol.

As I drove, I pulled out my phone and dialed. I only needed to wait a couple of rings before there was an answer.

"Hello?" the groggy voice said, surprisingly friendly considering I had just woken her up.

"Bri? Hi, this is Jason Hart. You were my son Jaxon's nurse back in August and September."

Immediately she sounded wide-awake. "Hi, Jason. What's wrong?"

"We're headed to the hospital right now. Jaxon has a fever that's pushing around 104. This isn't supposed to be happening, right?" I asked, praying she'd tell me that was normal for kids and everything was probably fine.

"No, that's not normal at all. He's only about six weeks

out of treatment, right?"

"Right."

I heard some rustling around in the background. "Listen, I'm going to call Debbie right now since she's the nurse practitioner over his care and can get through to everyone we need. She'll give the ER manager and security a heads up that you're coming so they can get you straight back. I'm heading up there now."

"Bri, you don't have to come up to the hospital," I argued, punching the gas to make it through a yellow light before it turned red.

"I don't have to," she said. "But I want to. I don't like when a recent patient has a setback like this, so I'd feel more comfortable being there."

"Well thank you."

"No problem. I'll see you in a bit." And she hung up.

Bri wasn't kidding when she said we would get straight back. When we drove up to the emergency room entrance twenty minutes later and walked through the door, security escorted us straight back to a private exam room while someone, who I assumed was a valet, went to park the car. I hadn't seen the setup down here before, but it was nice for an emergency room. There were probably twenty or so small and fully enclosed private rooms, each with a bed, a TV, and a sliding glass door so you could close out all the other ER noises.

I gently laid Jaxon down on the bed as Addison explained to the triage nurse his diagnosis and when his last treatment was. I was only halfway listening. I was scared. So scared. I thought we had gotten through the worst. I thought the fear and panic were over. But now it was all back again.

Within a few minutes, Jax was hooked up to an IV, he'd finally been given a dose of Tylenol, and several vials of blood had been drawn.

And then the waiting began.

I pretended to watch mindless TV without any volume while Jax slept, reaching over to check his forehead every once in a while. It took a couple hours, but his fever started to come down. Even I could tell it wasn't back to normal, but it was better.

Despite all the adrenaline, Addison couldn't stay awake either. She finally fell asleep, leaning on Jaxon's bed, arms folded beneath her head.

But me . . . My brain wouldn't shut down. Too many thoughts were racing around in there.

Is it just a virus?
Is the cancer back?
Are we looking at six more weeks in the hospital?

As much as I didn't want to know because I didn't want to deal with it, the wait was excruciating.

I quietly reached for my phone when I heard it ping in my pocket. It was Deuce.

Deuce: What's up, douchebag? Why am I sitting at the gym by myself? You stay up too late working out with the little lady?

I rolled my eyes. Leave it to Deuce to relate everything back to sex.

Me: At the hospital with Jax.
Deuce: Oh shit! What's wrong?
Me: Major fever. Running blood work now.
Deuce: Relapse?
Me: Don't know yet.
Deuce: Ok. I'll let Vanessa know so she can get all her praying people on it. Let me know if you need something.
Me: Thx

That was the thing about Deuce that most people didn't see. When he wasn't cracking jokes and being a perv, when life truly fell to shit, he was always willing to step up.

His text reminded me that I needed to let Adam and the coach know what was happening. Job or not, I wasn't leaving this hospital until we knew what was going on and everyone was situated.

As soon as I had sent my messages, I heard the sliding glass door open and the curtain rustle.

"Knock, knock," a voice said, and I immediately knew the news was not good.

"Come on in, Dr. Bates." I felt my entire body sag in defeat. Dr. Bates didn't work in the ER. There was only one reason he would be here. When Debbie and Bri followed him in, I knew we hadn't dodged a bullet like I had thought just a couple of weeks ago.

"Good morning, Jason," he said quietly. "How's he doing?"

"He still has a fever, but it's hovering around 100.5. So that's better, I guess." I rubbed my hand down my face as Dr. Bates rolled the circular stool over next to the bed and sat down. "You're here, so I'm guessing I need to wake Addison up for this discussion."

He flashed a small, compassionate smile. "That's probably a good idea."

I took a deep breath and closed my eyes momentarily, steeling myself for what was about to happen. Then I leaned over to stroke her hair. "Babe," I said in her ear. "Hey, you need to wake up." She stretched her arms, not fully waking up. "Babe, Dr. Bates is here to talk to us."

At that, her head popped up and she looked around. First at the doctor, then Debbie, then Bri, then back to the doctor.

Then she sagged against me in defeat. No one had to say a word. We knew.

"How bad?" she asked quietly as she grabbed my hand and clung to it for support.

"His neutrophil counts are low," Dr. Bates said. "Very low. Lower than when he was diagnosed. And his platelets are struggling, too."

"So it's back," I stated, knowing what the answer would be.

He nodded. "We won't know for sure to what degree until we do another biopsy. But yes, it appears that he is having a recurrence."

I put my arms around Addison and buried my face in her hair. I felt her begin to cry as tears slid down my own face as well. No one spoke while we stayed that way for several minutes. Once I finally felt myself in a little bit more control, I looked up.

I cleared my throat. "So what's, um . . . what's the plan now?"

"We're admitting him immediately," the doctor said. "With his counts so low, we don't want to waste any time. Debbie already has the diagnostic team back in place, getting prepared for whatever the biopsy shows."

I nodded.

"And Bri has already set up his room with Minecraft and hidden some squirt guns in the room," he added with a smile.

I nodded again. "Thank you."

"We'll give you guys a few minutes before we move you upstairs." And then they all walked out.

We sat in silence again for a few minutes. There wasn't really anything to say.

Finally, Addison sighed. "I guess we should call the family."

I nodded.

"I really don't want them to come to the hospital right now."

I nodded again.

"Do you think we could tell your mom and she could make all the phone calls? I don't think I can handle calling my parents."

I nodded one more time.

"Say something, Jason," she begged. "I don't like it when you're silent like this."

I opened my mouth and then closed it again as I pulled her closer to me. I sighed. "I'm so sorry, Addison," I finally whispered.

"Sorry?" she asked, looking at me with a confused expression on her face. "Why are you sorry? You didn't give him leukemia."

I shook my head, eyes filling with tears again. "I don't know why I'm sorry. Because I don't want you to have to go through this again. Because I'm your husband, and I already know I won't be by your side all the time while you sit in the hospital room with him." She began stroking my cheeks with her hands. "Because I feel like there should be something I can do to fix this, and there's not. I can't fix this, Addison, and I feel guilty because that's my job as your husband. That's my job as his dad. I'm supposed to fix this."

"Oh, baby," she said as she wiped the tears that had fallen off my cheeks with her thumbs. "That's how we all feel right now. We all feel out of control and restless and like there's something else we should be doing. But there's noth—Jason, look at me," she interrupted herself, moving her head around to make eye contact with me again when I looked away. When I finally looked at her again, she continued. "There's nothing *any* of us can do. Except hope and pray and follow doctor's orders. And be honest with me when you don't feel strong so I can help hold you up, too," she finished with a small smile.

"I'm supposed to be the strong one," I whispered. "I'm supposed to be holding you up."

"That's not what marriage is, babe. We have to hold each other up. My weaknesses are your strengths. My strengths are your weaknesses. Remember?"

I nodded, knowing she was right. I had to trust her with my feelings, too. I felt myself relax now that I had gotten some of it off my chest. I took a deep breath and wiped my face of all the moisture. "Thanks, babe. You're right."

"I'm sorry, I'm what?" she joked.

"Don't push it," I said with a small grin. I grabbed her hand and kissed her knuckles, grateful once again for this strong, amazing woman who had chosen to be by my side for the rest of our lives.

As we started to settle back into silence, there was another knock on the door and the curtain was pushed open.

"Okay," Bri said as she walked in with an orderly. "You guys ready to head back upstairs?"

We nodded and stood up, still clasping hands, prepared to help each other through the next stage of this nightmare.

Chapter NINETEEN

I pushed open the hospital room door and quietly dropped my bag next to the small bathroom. The only light on in the room came from a crack in the bathroom door. Addison and Jaxon were both sleeping, and I didn't want to disturb them. But after spending three days in Chicago, I was ready to be with them again.

I made my way over to the recliner Addison was asleep in and leaned over, hands on the armrests, and kissed her forehead gently. She stirred and opened her eyes, looking up at me.

"Jason," she breathed with a smile, wrapping her arms around my neck and pulling me down for a deeper kiss.

"Mmmmm," I moaned quietly. "I missed you so much," I said, still kissing her.

"I think I hate away games," she said as she kissed me back.

"Me too." After a few more minutes of getting reacquainted with my wife, I finally pulled away to rub my hand across her belly. "How are all my babies doing?"

"Depends on which one you're asking about." She shifted in the recliner to get more comfortable as I sat down on the chair next to her.

"Let's start with the easy one. How's this little man?" I leaned over and kissed her belly.

"Busy," she answered as she stroked her fingers through my hair.

"He keeping you up at night?" I kept rubbing her stomach, hoping he would kick hard enough that I could feel him.

"Nah. Mostly after I eat. Especially if it's sugar." She giggled.

I smiled. "I see that sweet tooth is finally back."

"Hey, what baby wants, baby gets."

I smiled at her, enjoying having a small moment of normalcy before addressing the more serious side of things. "How's Jax?" I asked, looking over at him as he slept. His face was starting to look too thin.

She sighed as she started rubbing her own stomach.

"Same. Fever comes and goes. Chemo makes him throw up. Same ol' same ol'."

I sighed and grabbed her hand. I hated having to leave town so often during all of this. Actually, I hated having to leave town so often in general. But it was just that much worse this season.

"And how are you holding up?" I asked as I stroked her knuckles and played with her fingers. "Did you leave this room at all while I was gone?"

"Um . . ." she said, crinkling her nose, pretending to ignore my question.

"Addison," I reprimanded. "You know it's not good for you to stay here all day every day. You need to get out and get some fresh air, too."

"I know, Jason," she said defensively. "But I don't want to leave him alone."

I raised an eyebrow, challenging her. "You're telling me Mick or my mom or even Samantha wouldn't come sit here with him for a couple hours while you go take a shower and get some sleep at home in a real bed?"

"I know, I know," she said with a grimace as she rolled onto her side. "It's just not the same when you're not here, okay? I promise I've been taking breaks to walk around the halls. And your mom has been keeping me stocked on 'pregnancy food,' as she calls it. So I'm okay." She grimaced again and couldn't seem to get comfortable.

"Addison, what's going on?" The way she kept holding her belly was throwing up some red flags. "Are you in pain?"

"It's not really pain," she said with a grunt. "He's just so active he's been hurting me a lot today."

"Explain hurting."

She rolled her eyes. "I'm not in labor, Jason. I know what that feels like."

"Well, what does *this* feel like?"

"I don't know how to describe it. It's just a deep pressure, really low in my belly. I'm sure it's normal for a second baby."

"Uh huh. And how's the bleeding."

She wouldn't look me in the eye when she said, "Fine."

"Addison . . ."

She sighed and shifted her body again. "What, Jason? There's nothing we can do, okay? Just drop it, I'm fine."

But as soon as the words were out of her mouth, she froze, and the look on her face said otherwise.

"Addison, what's wrong?"

"Um . . . I . . ." Her eyes went wide as she looked at me. "Can you help me to the bathroom?" she whispered.

I reached my arm around her and helped lift her under the shoulders. As soon as she moved, she groaned.

"What? What?" Something was very wrong now.

"That's not right. It's not supposed to hurt like that. Jason, something's wrong."

I immediately reached over and slammed my hand on the call button above Jaxon's head, hoping I didn't wake him up in my panic.

"Is everything okay, Addison?" Bri's voice said over the intercom.

"Bri, it's Jason. I need a wheelchair in here now. Something's wrong with the baby."

I heard the intercom click off as I put my focus back on my wife. Within seconds, Bri came racing in with the wheelchair. "What happened?" she asked, going into full nurse mode.

"I . . . I don't know," Addison said. "I've been hurting more than normal today, but just now it started—oooooh," she groaned.

"Oh yeah," Bri said as she helped me get Addison in the chair. "She needs to go to labor and delivery right now. Do you need me to come with you?"

"NO!" Addison said abruptly. "I need you to stay with Jaxon, Bri. Please! Please don't leave him."

"Ok, I'll do that," Bri said, reassuring her. "Go now, Jason. I'll call up there and tell them what's happening."

As we rushed through the halls and made our way onto the elevators, Addison just kept talking. "It's too early. This can't be happening. He's only twenty-four weeks. He's not big enough yet." I never responded. What could I say? It *was* too early. But I didn't have time to think too hard about it. As soon as the elevator doors opened on the labor and delivery floor, and we got to the registration desk, a nurse met us and hurried us into a room.

She was a young Asian woman with glasses. Her straight black hair was pulled back into a ponytail, and she looked like she was no-nonsense when it came to her job.

"Let's get you into this gown and then we'll get you checked out," she said, handing it to Addison. "Can you get dressed on your own, or do you need help?"

"I think Jason is gonna have to help me. I've been in some pain today. Can I use the bathroom while I'm in there?"

"Not yet," the nurse answered as she headed over to a laptop and opened what looked like a medical program. "Let's see what's happening first."

The bathroom was a lot bigger than the tiny one in Jaxon's room, so we were able to both fit in there without a problem. It took longer to get her undressed than normal because she would have to stop every once in a while when a pain took over. When I helped her slip her panties off, I froze.

There was blood. So much blood.

"Addison," I said slowly. "Baby."

She looked down, and her eyes widened. "That must have been the gush I felt when we were arguing," she whispered and caught my gaze.

"It's okay," I said calmly, then continued on with the task of getting her in the hospital gown. "We're already here. The doctor is on her way. It's gonna be fine," I said, trying to reassure myself as much as her. I tied the back of her gown and kissed her on the forehead. "Everything is fine, okay?"

She nodded, and I led her back out of the bathroom and into the bed.

After answering a whole list of questions about when the pains started and how her bleeding had been for the last couple of weeks, the doctor finally walked in the door.

"Well, you two are the last people I expected to see tonight," Dr. Plunkett said as she sat down on the rolling stool and rolled herself down by Addison's feet. "I'm glad I was already here delivering a baby." She took a look at the monitors above the nurse's head, squinted her eyes as she looked at the data. "When did you start feeling pain, Addison? Scoot your bottom down this way so I can check you."

"Um . . . yesterday, I guess?" she said as she maneuvered her way down the bed.

While they got situated, the nurse wrapped some sort of a monitor around Addison's waist. A few seconds later, we heard the sounds of the baby's heartbeat.

"Well, that's a very good sign," Dr. Plunkett said as she adjusted a sheet over Addison's legs and did whatever it is doctors do down there.

Addison grimaced, and I grabbed her hand.

A few seconds later, it was over. "Okay," Dr. Plunkett said while taking off her gloves and heading over to the sink to wash her hands. "It seems that you are in labor."

"What? It's too soon!" I said in a panic.

"Which is why she's going to be staying here with us for a little while," she said as she dried her hands and threw the paper towel away. "We'll give you a small dose of magnesium to try and stop the labor, but we'll need to monitor you for a while. However, that's not the part I'm the most worried about."

Addison and I looked at each other, and I grabbed her hand. It struck me as kind of ridiculous that we were getting so used to getting bad news that it became a habit to grab hands and brace ourselves for the worst.

"You're dilated to a four." Addison's head dropped to her

chest. I wasn't quite sure what that meant, but I knew it wasn't good. "I'm not sure why you're having this issue, being that your last pregnancy was normal. But I suspect you have a weak cervix."

"Is that what's causing the labor?" I asked.

"That's probably a good part of it. And the stress of everything else is exacerbating it."

I sat back and sighed again.

"Normally, under the circumstances, I wouldn't be able to say this, but you guys are so lucky you were already at the hospital when this happened. When a cervix fails, it happens rapidly. Most women don't make it to the hospital before the baby is born. We have a good chance of helping him stay put now, which is exactly what we want."

"I'm on bed rest for the rest of this pregnancy, aren't I?" Addison finally asked.

"I'm afraid so," the doctor said, patting her knee. "We need to do an ultrasound first though, to see whether or not you'll need a cerclage to keep your cervix intact, but I'm not gonna give you false hope. You're probably looking at getting the procedure done by this afternoon. I want to get your labor under control first."

As she and Addison chatted more, I started running the logistics in my head. If Addison was on bed rest, I needed to make sure Jaxon had someone at the hospital with him during the day when I was at work.

The sleep is going to be terrible, but I will, of course, be the one spending the nights with him. I have to see if my mom can maybe make up a schedule for the family to come stay with him when I'm out of town. Addison will need me, too, so maybe I can split my time between home and the hospital.

"Jason."

And the diagnostics team needs to know that any information they give her needs to be on an "as-needed" basis to help keep her stress levels down. I need to call Adam, Judy, Coach Ramiro, Addison's mom . . .

"Jason!"

"Huh," I answered, finally stopping long enough to realize Addison was talking to me.

"I said, why don't you head back over to Jaxon's room for the night. It's not like I'm going anywhere." I looked around and realized we were the only two people in the room. I had spaced so hard, I didn't see anyone else leave.

"Are you sure?"

She cracked half a smile. "Yeah. I'd rather you be there with him than here with me. I'll text you if anything happens."

I nodded and stood up, kissing her softly. "I love you," I said as I started rubbing her belly. "I love both of you."

"We love you, too," she answered. "Now get out of here before you tempt me to go back to his room myself."

"Yes, ma'am," I joked as I made my way toward the door. "I'll be back later this morning to check on you."

She smiled and blew me a kiss as I walked out the door.

My mind started racing again as I walked.

I should probably wait to call Mom until she's awake. I'm off tomorrow, so there's no use in waking her up now. There's nothing that can be done right now anyway. I should hire someone to do all the cooking and cleaning at home while Addison's on bed rest. That way I know she's getting fed, and there is someone there in case of an emergency. Maybe Vanessa knows someone. I think one of her sisters or cousins or someone's husband got laid off. Maybe they need the money. If Vanessa trusts them, I can trust them . . .

I was so exhausted from being on the road and because of

how late it was, but I couldn't shut my brain down. The feeling was overwhelming.

I walked into Jax's room to find Bri sitting next to him, e-reader open in her lap. She looked up as I walked in. "How'd it go?"

"Mandatory bed rest for the remainder of the pregnancy," I answered as I plopped onto the recliner Addison had been sitting in just an hour before.

"Early labor?"

"Yep."

"Giving her magnesium?"

"Yep."

"Too much stress?"

"Yep. And a weak cervix that is already dilated to a four." I rubbed my hands over my eyes, glad that she was a nurse, and I didn't need to explain everything in detail to her. I'd be doing enough of that when the family started getting calls.

"Are they doing a cerclage?"

"Ultrasound first to decide. But most likely."

She took a deep breath before speaking again. "I know my specialty is pediatric oncology. And I know that there is nothing good about having a child hospitalized for treatment, but in this case, I'm really glad he was here. If you'd been at home . . ."

"I know. That's exactly what the doctor said." I leaned over Jaxon's bed and started stroking his bald head as he slept.

"In a roundabout way, Jaxon sort of saved his brother's life tonight."

I smiled. "You hear that, buddy? Even while you're sleeping, you're a superhero. Just by being you." I kissed him on his forehead and settled back into the recliner, opening it up so I could stretch out. My legs still hung over the edge, but it was better than nothing.

"I'll let you get some sleep," Bri said. "I've got some coffee to drink and some charts to update."

"Yeah, what are you doing here, anyway? You don't usually work overnights."

"His regular night nurse is on vacation, and I don't like the nurse who took her shift," she said, stretching. "I'd rather pull an all-nighter or two on my days off than listen to Jax complain about how awful she is."

I chuckled. "Well thanks for that, Bri. We appreciate you more than you know."

She smiled and ducked out of the room, leaving me to my son and my thoughts. It took a couple hours for my brain to finally wear itself out. But it finally did, and I fell into what was arguably the worst night's sleep of my life.

Chapter TWENTY

I hated away games with a passion. I'd never hated them before. Not like this. But I hated them now.

I hated having to get on an airplane with a bunch of teammates and fly so far from home.

I hated staying in a hotel, knowing the rest of my family was sleeping in hospital beds.

I hated looking out into the crowd and seeing smiling, happy families while mine was falling apart.

I hated that I couldn't keep my head in the game. I was trained to keep my head in the game. I was trained to focus. I used to be able to block out everything else. It was one of my strengths. But now? Now the blocks were knocked down, and everything was a distraction. Crowds. Groupies. Media. I noticed everything now.

"You alright, man?" Deuce asked after we went through team warm-ups.

"Peachy," I deadpanned as I picked up a football and started tossing it back and forth with Mason, trying to go through my normal pre-game routine.

"Why don't you have your Beats in?" he asked.

"Can't find them. Think they're at the hospital."

"Do you want to use mine?" he offered. I avoided looking at him, knowing I was going to see concern written all over his face.

"Nope. Doesn't help anyway."

"Did you get any more updates today?"

"Don't wanna talk about it, Deuce. I'm trying to focus."

"Okay," he said, hands up in a defensive pose as he backed away. "You know where to find me if you need me."

I nodded and threw the ball back to Mason, glad that he had taken over as one of my training partners. He never asked me questions or tried to talk to me about the shit-storm that had become my life. He talked shop with me, and that was it.

I went through the rest of the pre-game warm-ups in a fog. My concentration level was shot, so I just went through the motions. Even Deuce's attempts at pumping up the team in the locker room didn't work on me. Usually, I was the first one in the mix. This time, though, it wasn't happening. I was done. I didn't have anything else to give except the bare minimum.

"Hart!" Coach called as we all ran for the tunnel.

"Yeah, Coach."

"You got your head in this game?"

"Yes, sir."

"You know all that anger you're feeling right now? How pissed off you are at everything going on around you?"

"Yes, sir."

"You know what to do with it. Focus and use it to your advantage."

I nodded and followed my team through the tunnel. The cheers unnerved me. The National Anthem unnerved me. They even ran the Hart to Heart public service announcement at one point, which unnerved me. I knew if I didn't get my focus back and get some aggression out, I was liable to crack right here. During this game.

By the second quarter, we were down by seven points. I wasn't playing as well as I normally did, and I knew it. My teammates knew it too. So did the other team.

We lined up on the thirty-seven-yard line when I came face to face with their offensive lineman, Brandon Gonzales. He was the same jackass who had insulted Addison a couple of years ago, pissing me off so bad it had led to the play of my life and a touchdown by yours truly.

I smirked as I felt the aggression boil through me. If anyone could get me riled up and back in the game, it was him.

"Got any more shit to say about my wife?" I taunted. He kept his eyes focused and wouldn't look at me. "What's the matter, douchebag? Afraid you're gonna just piss me off and give me the energy I need to take you down?"

He finally looked up at me, and I saw it. He wasn't keeping his mouth shut because he was afraid it would feed my skill level. He was keeping his mouth shut out of pity.

And that's when I finally snapped.

"What's the matter? Don't you have anything to say to me, mother fucker!" I yelled at him.

I heard his quarterback yelling plays and felt everyone move around me. I knew in the back of my mind that I had a job to do and a play to follow through with, but I couldn't get that part of me to catch up with the part that was so enraged.

I went after Gonzales and got him down in a quick tackle. But instead of getting up and going after the quarterback, I stayed down, hands gripping his jersey, shaking him with all my might and screaming in his face. "What's the matter, you big piece of shit? Don't have anything to say? Too busy feeling sorry for me to do your job? Talk shit to me, mother fucker! DO YOUR FUCKING JOB!"

I heard the whistles long after the play was over and finally felt myself being pulled off of him.

"HART!" Coach yelled from the sidelines. "GET YOUR ASS OFF THE FIELD!"

I ripped my helmet off my head and walked over to the bench, throwing my helmet at the water cooler before plopping myself down on the bench, head in my hands. I was trying desperately to control my breathing.

"Mason! Get out there!" Coach yelled before turning on me. "I don't know what the fuck that was out there, Hart, but if you can't get your shit together, you won't be stepping foot on that field. That just earned us a fifteen-yard penalty. You hear me!"

I nodded but kept my head down. I was losing it, and there was nothing I could do to stop it.

I made my way into Addison's hospital room later that evening. Good thing it had been a morning game in San Francisco. No telling how late I would have been if we had played any later.

"Hi babe," I said with a smile as I leaned over to kiss her. "How are you?"

"Mmm . . . I'm shaky and restless," she answered. "But I'm hanging in there."

"Magnesium still making you shaky?"

"Yeah," she said. "But I'm okay."

"Did you watch the game?" I asked as I sat down and brushed her hair back behind her ear. I missed being close to her so badly. I couldn't stop touching her if I tried.

"I did," she nodded. "But I figured I'd wait for you to bring it up before asking why you didn't play the entire second half."

I shrugged, still kind of embarrassed about the whole thing. I wasn't embarrassed about attacking Gonzales. He wasn't known for being a nice guy on or off the field, so whatever. What I was embarrassed by was not doing my job the way I was supposed to. The way I was used to. I had let down my coaches, my team, and my fans. And now I realized I had let down my wife as well.

"Jay," she said, running her fingers through my hair. "You know they have really good chaplains here at the hospital. And therapists that work in conjunction with the oncology department."

I scoffed. "I don't need therapy, Addison. I just needed to be with my family, okay? It was a bad game, that was all."

"Okay," she said. "I just worry about you."

I smiled at her. "Thanks, babe," I said, kissing her knuckles. "But stop. I'm the one taking care of you right now."

"Have you gone to see Jax yet?"

I shook my head. "Mick is with him, so I wanted to come see you first. Did you talk to Dr. Bates while I was gone?"

"No," she said with a sigh. "Bri stopped by to give me an update though."

"And?"

"No change. His counts keep fluctuating, but it's not even close to where it needs to be."

"Shit," I mumbled as I closed my eyes. "It's been almost a month. I wonder if we're gonna be changing his meds soon."

"I hope so," she whispered. I looked at her as her eyes started to well up with tears.

"Hey." I put my arms around her and pulled her as close to me as I could get with the bed railing in the way. "What's wrong? Why are you crying?"

"I haven't seen him in a week, Jason. It's killing me." That's when her sobs began. All I could do was hold her while she cried. It was an impossible situation. She was on mandated bed rest. He was too sick to even use the bathroom, so using a wheelchair to get to her was out of the question. There really was no solution for this situation.

A short time later, Dr. Plunkett came into the room. She shot us a compassionate smile before sitting down.

"How are you feeling?" she asked Addison.

"Shaky. Restless. Terrified that I'm missing something important by being stuck here instead of in Jaxon's room."

"Sounds about right," Dr. Plunkett said. "Any unusual pain?"

"Nothing I haven't already told you about. Is there any way I'll be getting out of here anytime soon?"

"That's actually what I came in here to talk to you about." She pulled up Addison's information on the computer before continuing her thought. "You've been here for about a week, so we've had a really good time frame to monitor you."

Addison nodded. "Yeah, there hasn't been much alone time, that's for sure."

"It can get pretty daunting. I recognize that." She rolled away from the computer and over to Addison's bedside. "The good news is that the baby seems to be doing well. He's growing at a healthy rate. He's not in distress. He's doing fabulous."

I breathed a sigh of relief. This was the one bit of good

news we'd had in a long time.

"That's such a relief," Addison said. "As long as he's doing well, I can hang on until he's big enough to be born."

"I'm glad to hear you say that," the doctor said. "The cerclage seems to be doing its job, but the only way it will keep working is if you stay on one hundred percent bed rest until it's time to deliver."

"Is there any way I can be set up to do bed rest in Jaxon's room?" Addison asked quickly. "I mean, I know that's not standard procedure or anything, but we can see if they'll move the recliner out and a cot in or something since the recliner won't lay flat enough for me. We could do that, right? Instead of me going home?" she asked, seeming pleased by the idea. She had obviously thought it through while I was gone.

"Well, that's the thing," Dr. Plunkett interrupted. "I can't release you to go back home at this point."

"Why not? I . . . I don't understand," Addison said. "You just said the baby was healthy and the cerclage was holding."

"But your labor hasn't completely stopped."

"She hasn't had labor pains in a week, though," I said, feeling really confused now.

"That's because of the magnesium," she explained. "Every time we decrease the amount of magnesium to wean you off of it, your body shows signs that it's going right back into labor. With a weak cervix, cerclage or not, we can't risk taking you off the IV drip."

Addison's head fell back onto the pillow as mine dropped forward. One step forward, three more steps back.

"So I have to stay here, in this room, in this bed, away from my son, who is going through chemotherapy, so I can save a baby I've never met. Is that right?" Addison said quietly, her voice laced with anger.

"I'm sorry," Dr. Plunkett said. "I know this is not the news you were wanting. We're going to start giving you steroid shots to help the baby's lungs develop faster. I don't anticipate you're going to carry this baby to term, so we want to get him as ready as possible."

"Thanks, doc," I said as Addison just stared at the ceiling.

"You're welcome." She stood up and headed for the door. "I'll come check on you again tomorrow. In the meantime, if you need anything, let me know."

I nodded at her as she left and turned back to Addison.

"I know this is the world's worst thing to say, and you might hate me for it," she said, looking at me with a blank stare, "but I don't know this baby. I love this baby, but I don't know him. I know *Jaxon*. I feel like I have to choose between them. Either keep this one safe and lose Jax or be there for Jax and lose this one."

I tried to interrupt her, but she stopped me. "Jay, if they make me choose—if I have to choose between the two of them—I choose Jaxon. I don't know this baby yet. I choose Jaxon." Then she rolled over so her back was facing me, and I knew she had hit her limit too.

Seeing her like this—defeated, angry, restless—it confirmed to me what I had to do.

We had officially been backed into a corner. That meant the one thing I swore I would never give up for anything was about to be the biggest sacrifice I had ever had to make.

"Thanks for meeting me today, Coach," I said as I sat down in the hard chair across the desk from him. "I know it's your day off."

He nodded. "It is, but frankly, after your performance yesterday, I was already anticipating your call."

I grimaced as I rubbed my hands down my face, gathering my thoughts. He was right about my performance. But we'd get to that later.

"What's the update, son? Tell me about your family. I need to know what's going on before we get to the main part of this conversation."

I looked up and realized he probably already knew why I was here. So I told him everything.

I told him about Jaxon's chemo not working like last time. I told him how every time I went out of town I came back to a child that looked more and more sick. I told him about Addison's labor, the steroids she was taking, and her mandatory hospitalization. I told him about the recliner I slept in every night and the spreadsheet my mother had tacked to a cork board in Jaxon's room, telling me who was going to stay with him while I was at work. I told him how sick I was of seeing the pity in everyone's eyes the minute I walked into the locker room and how much worse it was to know everyone was walking on eggshells around me.

And I told him how when even Brandon Gonzales, who prided himself on his trash talk, wouldn't look me in the eye without giving me a look of pity, I lost it. I laid it all on the line for Coach . . . everything that was happening and everything I was feeling.

By the time I was done, there were tears streaming down my face and my voice was cracking when I spoke. I felt like the biggest pussy.

He sat back and absorbed everything I had said before responding.

"How much time off are you asking for, son?" he finally asked once I had pulled myself back together. He did know why I was here.

"Ideally? The remainder of the season."

He nodded. "You realize you're under a multi-year contract."

"Yes sir," I answered. "Obviously, at minimum, Addison will be out of the hospital by next training camp. And, fingers crossed, Jaxon will be on the mend too. Don't have a clue yet about the baby. We'll take that as it comes."

He nodded again, steepling his fingers as he leaned against the desk. "I'll put in a call with HR about how it affects your pay and all that. Since we're only talking six weeks and the playoffs, I'm guessing it'll fall under some sort of family/medical leave act or something."

I nodded.

"Are you sure you want to do this? It's always possible the organization will want to renegotiate your contract instead, and that might not work in your favor."

"I know," I said, feeling resolved. I loved football. But I loved my family more. After everything we had been through lately, there was nothing I was more sure of in my life. "But I need to be there with them. I'm the head of my household, and I have to do this. I don't want it to cost me my career. I love my job. But I have to take that risk."

"I respect that," he said, standing up and putting out his hand to shake mine. "And I'll make sure the organization knows I'm in agreement with your decision. You're stretched too thin, and this is keeping your priorities straight. Get through all this shit. I want you back for next season."

"Thank you, sir," I said, shaking his hand. "Just have HR put in a call to Adam with any details they need to work out. I trust him with all my contracts. And I'm busy with a few things right now, so I'll let him take care of that part."

"Will do. Give Addison a hug from me. We'll keep praying, man."

"I appreciate it."

With that, I walked out the door.

Next stop, the hospital.

Where I had to tell my wife her husband was unemployed.

Chapter TWENTY-ONE

"The good news," Dr. Bates said, "is that his counts are relatively steady. They're low. Much lower than we'd like, but they don't appear to be dropping."

"What exactly does that mean?" Addison asked from her hospital bed. She wasn't even allowed to leave her bed to go to the oncology wing for meetings about Jax's treatment. Fortunately, Dr. Bates didn't seem to have any qualms about coming to the maternity ward as needed.

"It means that what little immune system he has is trying its darndest to fight the cancer cells," he answered. "They're not making much progress, but it's definitely an impressive effort."

"And it gives the chemo a chance to do its job, right?" she asked hopefully.

"Well, that's the bad news," he responded somberly and then sighed. "Jaxon's body is no longer responding to any of the treatments."

"Shit," I mumbled under my breath as I rubbed my hand

down my face.

"What do you mean he's not responding?" Addison asked, starting to sound frantic. "So try another drug! There are lots of them out there. You just have to find the right one!"

"Hey, hey, hey," I said, reaching over and rubbing my hand down her hair. "Don't panic yet, okay? Look at me, Addison." She looked over, and I saw the panic that was setting in. "You know what Dr. Plunkett said about stressing your body out."

"But Jason—"

"I know," I interrupted her gently. "I know. But we haven't heard everything he has to say yet. And we don't want to have two boys in the hospital, right?"

She nodded.

"Okay, take a deep breath, baby," I instructed, and I took a deep breath with her. "You okay?" She nodded. "You ready to hear more?" She nodded again.

"I'm sorry, Dr. Bates," Addison said more calmly. "Apparently all the magnesium and everything else they're giving me is heightening some of my anxiety. I feel so much more emotional than normal, so just ignore me when I start to panic."

Dr. Bates smiled at her as he fidgeted with the stethoscope around his neck. "I'm used to heightened anxiety, Addison. Please don't think I find it a weakness. It's part of the job when you work in oncology. As I was saying, Jaxon's body isn't responding to the chemo anymore. And at this point, we've maxed out all the available treatment options."

"So, what? He's just . . . he's . . . Are you saying he's terminal?" I asked, terrified of the answer.

"It doesn't look good," he said. "But I wouldn't call him terminal yet. Like I said, his body isn't declining, and as long as we can keep him that way, it buys us time to find a bone marrow match."

That seemed really ironic to me. Eighty thousand people registered to be bone marrow donors when Hart to Heart had done the nationwide stadium events. Matches were being made all over the place. Even Mason Hayes matched someone and was doing further testing to make sure his donation was a go.

Only Jaxon wasn't one of the lucky ones. He had zero matches out of all those people. There were still more applications that had to be processed because of the huge influx of people. But the chances were slim at this point, and we all knew it.

"How much time will it buy us?" Addison asked.

"I don't know the answer to that," the doctor answered. "The way the leukemia has spread . . . I don't like it. But as long as his body is maintaining where it's at, I'm cautiously optimistic."

He stopped and let us process all the information he'd just given us.

The leukemia has spread.

Cautiously optimistic.

It was a lot of conflicting information, but at least it wasn't all bad news.

"What about cord blood?" I asked.

"What do you mean?" Addison asked me, but I kept looking at Dr. Bates.

"Siblings have a better chance of matching bone marrow than anyone else, right? I know this baby is only a half brother, but what if his cord blood could be used?"

"Sounds like you've been doing your research," Kristina, our research nurse, said as she walked in the door. "Sorry I'm late. I was stuck on the phone."

"There's not a whole lot to do around here," I said. "So I started looking into other possible options. What can I say? I was bored and desperate to help."

"Well, it's funny you should mention it," she said as she pulled up a chair and sat down.

"Why is it funny I mentioned that?" I asked. "You've thought about cord blood, too, haven't you?"

"I have. But I wanted to make sure I had all my ducks in a row before presenting the idea. Every patient is different, ya know, so I wanted to make sure it was a viable option."

"So wait," Addison said, adjusting herself to a more comfortable position. "We'd use the cord blood for what? Instead of a bone marrow transplant?"

"Essentially, yes." Kristina shuffled through some papers as she spoke. "Assuming the cord blood was a close enough match to Jaxon, we'd do a cord blood transplant instead of a bone marrow transplant."

"Well, why haven't we thought of this before?" Addison asked excitedly.

"Because it's not a mainstream treatment," Kristina said. "Cord blood is still used on an experimental basis, and there are quite a few hoops that have to be jumped through before we can get legal clearance to do it. And that's *if* it's compatible with Jaxon's body."

I felt Addison's attitude deflate.

"What kind of hoops?" I was willing to jump through anything if it gave Jaxon a shot.

"I'm going to have to clear it with the Institutional Review Board and the CDC," she explained. "That could take some time. I'll have to pitch it to them as an experimental treatment and provide documentation that Jaxon is out of options and time. So it will be considered a 'single patient access' treatment."

"Assuming the cord blood is compatible with Jaxon's body," I said.

"Assuming it's compatible with Jaxon's body," she confirmed.

I took a deep breath. "How long does it normally take for this review board and the CDC to decide?"

"It can take a while. But that's why I was on the phone," she said excitedly. "I may have a contact at the CDC. It turns out, a college friend's father is a higher up over there. Not as high as I'd like, but high enough that I can plead our case. And don't be offended, but I'm going to play the celebrity card with him. If it works and I can get him to push our paperwork through to the next level quickly, I expect you to add a statement in all of your press releases about how pleased you are with how much they cared about your case."

Addison and I both nodded. "Of course. Whatever you want me to say. I can jump through that political hoop."

"Good. I'm going to get everything typed up and ready to go. I'll run it through them before the baby is born so they are aware of what's coming. The minute Baby Boy is here, we'll be putting a rush order in to test that cord blood. Assuming it comes back compatible, the official request for experimental treatment will be faxed over that day."

I took a deep breath, sat up straight, and looked over at Addison. "How ya feeling about that?" I asked her. She looked like I felt . . . a little deer-in-the-headlights.

"I think that's a whole lot of things that have to fall into place all at once," she said. "But it sounds like our best chance."

"I agree."

"Great," Kristina said. "Obviously there's going to be paperwork I will need you guys to sign. But in the meantime, I'm going to keep looking for other treatment options, and I'll find you as soon as I need your signatures. Sound good?"

"Yep," I responded, at the same time Addison said, "Absolutely."

"Okay. Then I'll be back as soon as I can." Kristina breezed out the door as quickly as she had arrived.

"Did you know about this?" I asked Dr. Bates.

"I knew she was working on it and researching what we needed," he said with a smirk. "But she's always researching options. Some of them work out. Some of them don't. It's best to let her break the news when it's set in stone." I nodded in understanding. "How's the pregnancy going, anyway, Addison?"

"Pretty miserable, actually," she chuckled. "The magnesium to stop my labor makes me shaky almost all of the time. And lying flat twenty hours out of the day makes it very hard to read or watch TV. Not to mention it's uncomfortable and obnoxious."

Dr. Bates smiled. "Yep. Women are definitely the tougher of the two sexes. Sometimes it takes situations like this to confirm that opinion."

"I agree," I said. "She's doing really great in here. I'm really proud of her for hanging in there."

She smiled over at me and laid her head back on the pillow. She looked exhausted. But I wasn't sure if it was physically or mentally that was making her so tired.

"Well, I'm going to head on out now," Dr. Bates said, standing up and heading toward the door. "I'll let you know if there are any major changes, Addison. But just know, Jason is doing a fine job of taking care of your boy. You can rest easy knowing that."

"Thank you, Dr. Bates," she replied. "I knew I picked a good one."

He chuckled as he walked out the door. As he left, I turned to look my wife in the eyes and gauge how she was really feeling about the situation.

"You okay?" I asked.

She took a deep breath and thought for a moment. "There are so many ways to answer that. Not quite terminal. God, Jay, that scares me. Like, *really* scares me," she said with tears in her eyes. "But then to know his body is fighting so hard makes me proud. And knowing we have this new option for treatment makes me feel hopeful. And knowing it's almost our last remaining hope has me wanting to start eating organic or something. I know that sounds ridiculous," she said sheepishly. "But I just feel this pressure to do everything right now. To make sure everything goes right with this pregnancy so we have the healthiest cord blood we can possibly have."

"You do realize either the cord blood is going to match or it's not, right?" I put my hand on her face and rubbed my thumb over her cheek. "There's nothing you could do or not do that will change that."

"I know." She put her hand over mine. "I didn't say it was a realistic feeling. Or rational. Maybe it's more panic than anything."

I grabbed her chin between my fingers and thumb, and I leaned in to brush my lips across hers. "What can I do to make it better? What do you need from me?"

She sighed. "Can you just climb in bed with me and hold me for a little while? I just need you to hold me. I miss you."

She scooted over slowly as I climbed on the bed with her, trying not to bump any wires or jar her any more than was necessary. It was slow going, and I was way too big for the bed. But we finally got situated with her back to my front, spooning. It was our favorite position, and I knew if the nurse didn't kick me out of the bed soon, I'd probably fall asleep.

We lay there quietly, just enjoying the feel of each other. I ran my hand over her ever-growing belly, thinking about my baby boy and wondering what he would be like. Would he look like me? Would he be smart? Or funny? Or athletic? The possibilities of who he would be were just endless, and it was kind of exciting to think about.

All of a sudden, I felt a thump in her stomach. "What the hell was that?" I asked.

Addison started giggling. "I think you just felt your first kick."

I kept my hand still when I felt it again. "Holy shit! Does he do that a lot?"

"Usually at night he starts bumping around. I didn't realize he was strong enough for you to feel it yet. But I guess the timing is about right."

I held my breath as he continued to kick around. Addison moved my hand anytime he rolled around somewhere else. It was the most amazing thing I had ever felt. "I think he's gonna be a placekicker, Addison! He's strong!"

"Or a soccer player."

"Now that's just not funny," I said with a stern voice.

She laughed. "He will be whatever he wants to be. He's a Hart. They're pretty stubborn."

I kissed her neck and breathed her in. "Yeah. We kind of are. And I'll love him no matter what he decides to be."

He thumped around for a little while longer until, I guess, he finally fell asleep. I was so content in the moment and so comfortable with my arms around Addison, it wasn't long before I fell asleep as well, proving there is truth to the phrase "like father, like son". Yeah. This baby was definitely a Hart.

Chapter TWENTY-TWO

Eight weeks. For eight weeks, Addison had been stuck in one wing of the hospital while Jaxon was stuck in another.

Fifty-six days. For fifty-six days, I'd been trying my damnedest to hold it all together. I'd been going back and forth between rooms, sleeping on a cot-sized recliner, eating shitty hospital food, making all medical decisions, comforting them both.

Three holidays. Thanksgiving. Christmas. New Year's. Split between the two of them. Trying to keep spirits up and show them a little bit of joy in this madness.

I didn't know how much longer I could hold myself together. One of them was trying not to die. The other was desperately trying to help someone new live. And I was stuck in the middle, trying not to crack.

I was angry. So angry. At the doctors. At God. At myself. At both of them. There was no rational reason for me to be angry with anyone. Cancer happens. Pregnancy complications happen. But all of it at once . . . it was too much. And if I didn't feel angry at someone, I'd fall into grief, and I didn't have the luxury to do that.

I took another deep breath as my head was in my hands, elbows on my knees. I'd been staring at a crack in the linoleum for a good while, but no matter how many breaths I took, I couldn't seem to get the anger under control.

Football had always been a stress reliever. Feel frustrated by everyday life? Take it out on the field. Get angry about the injustices of the world? Take it out on the field. Feel like your entire body is about to implode because you are stuck as the middleman between not one, but two impossibly stressful situations? Oh yeah . . . take a leave of absence so you have no outlet.

Rationally, I knew there was no way I could work during all of this. But the angry part of me was pissed at myself for giving up my one outlet. The one thing I'd been using as a coping mechanism for all these years.

I heard the door open but didn't look up. I was still too angry at the world to care, and as mad as I was, I didn't want to snap anyone's head off. Especially Bri. She'd been great to all of us. But I was still mad at her for being able to go home at night and sleep in a real bed and eat real food and have a life outside this *goddamn hospital.*

So it was better to not look up.

"Jason, honey?"

I really couldn't look up now, knowing it was my mom. I couldn't find any real reason to be mad at her except she wasn't here as much as I was, and I was just mad at anyone who wasn't here as much as I was. That didn't mean I wanted her to see me like this, though.

I felt her sit down in the chair next to me and rest her hand on my thigh.

"Stop shaking."

"I can't."

"Why not?"

"Because if I stop, my entire insides are going to combust in one giant fireball of anger."

"Now, Jason," she said calmly. "Don't you think that's just a tiny bit dramatic?"

I blew out a breath and looked up at her. "I'm about to lose it, Mom. I don't know what to do anymore. Where I'm supposed to be. Who I'm supposed to stay with. I know you and Rick and the rest of the family have been supportive, but I feel like I'm doing this on my own, and I'm about ready to say 'fuck it' and walk out on it all."

She began rubbing my back as she spoke. "Well, first of all, I know you aren't going to walk out on your family. I know you better than that. But I *do* think you need to get out of this hospital for a while. Take a day for yourself. Go home. Shower. Sleep. Rest. You are physically and mentally exhausted."

"Oh yeah, so just leave my son who is . . . who is . . . who is sick, and my wife, who could go into early labor at any moment here, so I can go rest? I promised I'd stay with Jax. I promised her I wouldn't leave him by himself. I can't go back on that. You know this. We've talked about this." It wasn't the first time this conversation had come up in the last eight weeks.

"Honey," Mom said, looking at me like I wasn't very smart. "Addison was panicking when she asked that of you. She was hormonal, scared for Jaxon, scared for the baby, scared for herself. She didn't mean for you to be here twenty-four hours a day until she has this baby! She doesn't want you to cause your own health to fail by running yourself into the ground."

"Ma," I said, sitting back in my chair. I'm sure I looked as exhausted as I felt. "I can't just leave him. Even if he's not by himself. What if something happens? What if . . . what if . . ."

"What if he takes a turn for the worse and you're not here with him?" she asked, knowing exactly what I was trying to say. I nodded. "Then you'd get a phone call and you'd be back up here in a matter of minutes. Jason," she said, shifting her body to look straight at me. "If the doctor thought Jaxon was going to pass away in the next few days, he would tell you. They don't let that go willy-nilly. There are signs and things the body does that are clues the end is near. Yes, Jaxon is very, very sick. And yes, he may be dying. But he isn't dying today. Or tomorrow, for that matter. And no one will fault you for getting a good night's rest in a real bed so you can be strong again tomorrow."

I rubbed my hands down my face in frustration. "How the hell did this even happen, Ma? How did I get married and have a kid one second and the next they're both hospitalized? What the hell did I ever do to deserve this kind of karma, huh? I can count the number of times I've slept in the same bed with my wife since we got married. Do you know what that feels like? I can't go back to that house right now without them there. There's nothing that would make me feel better right now, except maybe to punch God in the face."

"Jason Allen Hart, you stop that," she admonished. "I know you are angry right now at everyone and everything. But you seem to forget that all of this is temporary. *Temporary,*" she emphasized. "Sooner or later, that baby is coming, and then Addison will be out of the hospital. Either Jaxon will get better or he won't, and I'm praying he will, but you act like this limbo is the rest of your life! Yes, I know it's hard right now. I know you miss football and your teammates and your workouts. You have run yourself into the ground and have resisted leaving this building for the last eight weeks, trying to keep a promise that you yourself exaggerated the meaning behind. But you are doing no one any good anymore by trying to shoulder it all yourself. So here's what we're going to do," she said, grabbing her phone out of her purse. "We're going to have a family meeting. All hands on deck. And *you* are not going to be spending every night in this hospital anymore. A few nights a week? Of course. But we're setting up a schedule, and everyone will be helping out. Sound good?"

I hesitated. I didn't feel right not being here when my family was here and needed me, but I wasn't doing them much good either. Maybe she was right. Maybe it was time to let go a little and trust that nothing major would happen without me.

I nodded as she got to work, texting the entire family about the meeting we would be having in the great room down the hall.

As I sat, still lost in thought, there was a soft knock at the door. Bri's head popped in.

"Hey Jason," she said quietly, trying not to disturb Jax, who was napping. Again. "The maternity ward just called. You need to get up there."

I jumped to my feet, feeling the blood drain from my face. "What's wrong?"

She smiled at me. "Addison's water broke. It's time."

"But it's too early," I said, turning back to look at my mom, not quite sure what to do. "He's not supposed to be here for seven more weeks. It's too early!" I could feel the panic in my voice.

"Jason," my mom said calmly, standing up and putting her hands on my cheeks. "If the doctors say it's time, then it's what's best for everyone. Addison has been getting steroid injections for weeks just in case this happened. The baby is gonna be fine."

"What about Jax?" I asked. "I can't just leave him."

"You can," she said. "And you will. I'm right here with him, and as much as I'd love to be closer to you when my new grandson is born, I can wait until Mick gets here."

"Okay," I said, kissing her on the cheek. "Thanks, Ma." I turned and bent over to kiss Jax on the head. "I'll be back soon to tell you all about your baby brother," I whispered. As I headed toward the door, a thought occurred to me. "Bri, can you call . . ."

"I already called her," she interrupted. "Kristina is getting everyone in place to get the cord blood for testing now and is faxing the paperwork over to the CDC as we speak."

"Thanks," I said, and I rushed past her, down the hall and to the elevators. It took less than five minutes to get to Addison's room, but when I barged in, I had apparently missed a lot already.

"Jason!" Addison said through tears, her hands clenching the railing so hard her knuckles were white. "He's not supposed to be here yet, Jason! Make them give me something to stop it!" she cried.

"Jason," the doctor said, "her water broke, and there's nothing we can do to stop the contractions. We can't give her that much magnesium, and it wouldn't do any good anyway. There is as major risk of infection to the baby if we don't deliver soon. He's as ready as he's going to be. We can't wait."

I rushed to Addison's bedside and grabbed her hand, kissing her knuckles as she squeezed.

"I'm sorry, Jason. I didn't mean it," she cried when I grabbed her hand.

"What are you talking about, babe?" A dozen people milled about, setting up equipment and racing around like they were preparing for the worst-case scenario.

"I didn't mean it when I said I would choose Jaxon over the baby," she said as tears ran down her face. "I can't choose. I would never be able to choose. I'm so sorry! Please, God, make it stop! I'm sorry!"

"Hey, hey, hey," I said, brushing her tears away with my free hand. "Those were just words you said when you were mad, okay? I know you didn't mean that you wanted something bad to happen, okay? I just told my mom I wanted to punch God in the face. You think I meant that?"

She hiccupped through her tears and shook her head, visibly calming down.

"Exactly. I know you're scared, baby. But he's had a lot of steroids to help his lungs grow. He's gonna be fine." I wouldn't let her know I was just as scared as she was. She needed me now, and I could be strong for a little while longer. I had to be. "Can you trust me on this?"

She looked into my eyes, took a deep breath, and nodded.

"Okay. Then let's have a baby."

Just then, she squeezed my hand tighter than I had ever felt, and an almost feral-sounding moan came out of her mouth.

"Push through it, Addison," the doctor said. "The stronger you push, the faster this is over."

"I can't!" she resisted. "Please! It hurts so bad!"

"Doesn't she have an epidural?" I asked, surprised that she was in so much pain. I honestly thought that would have been done already.

"The labor came on too quickly," the doctor explained, still keeping her eyes underneath the blue sheet that was draped over Addison's legs. "Even if we could get the anesthesiologist here in the next couple of minutes, the epidural wouldn't even kick in until after the delivery. Here comes another one. Push, Addison!"

I held her hand and one leg like they had shown me as a nurse counted to ten. The contractions seemed to be coming closer together. Or at least my hand was getting squeezed a lot more. I wasn't sure what to do, so I just kept encouraging her and kissing her knuckles as I watched the woman I loved more than anything in this world suffer through the most unimaginable pain I had ever seen. And I admit . . . I felt like the world's biggest pussy.

For years, I had done my own share of complaining about injuries. Twisted knees, broken fingers, massive bruises. But this . . . this was on a whole different level of pain. Addison was literally being gutted from the inside out. I would never, ever look at her the same way again. She was the rock star when it came to pain . . . not me.

"One more push, Addison. He's almost here," the doctor said. "Jason, come down here closer. You're about to see your son be born."

I hesitated, not wanting to leave Addison. But she didn't even seem to notice I was there. She was too focused on what she was doing.

With one final scream, I watched as Addison pushed our son out of her body and into the doctor's arms.

Holy.

Shit.

I couldn't take my eyes off of him. He was the smallest thing I'd ever seen in my life. Like a tiny little kitten or something. Except he was covered in blood and this white goo.

"It's a boy!" the doctor announced, holding him up for us

to see. Before we could even react, the baby was whisked out of her arms by a waiting nurse, who took him straight to a tall table covered with a blue sheet. I'm not even sure who cut his umbilical cord. Someone else then moved right next to the doctor, ready with some vials and other medical paraphernalia.

"Don't forget the cord blood," Addison whispered, sounding as exhausted as she looked.

"Oh, we haven't forgotten," the person with the vials answered. "As soon as the placenta passes, we'll have everything we need to get that ball rolling."

Seconds later, the baby was being rolled out of the room. Addison hadn't even held him yet.

"Where are they taking him?" I asked. I had never done this before, and I wasn't sure what I was supposed to do. I felt like a dumbass.

"They're taking him to the NICU," said one of the nurses, who had stopped what she was doing to come around the bed and talk to me. "I know that was a really quick introduction to your son. Much quicker than we like. But with him being so premature, we need to get him to the NICU as soon as possible."

"Is he going to be all right?" I asked, for the first time feeling real fear that his life might be in danger, too. Not anxiety like I had been feeling. But fear.

"He actually looked really good," she said. "His color was good. His APGAR scores were excellent, considering his gestational age. Of course, they'll know more once they get him settled in. But he didn't show any additional warning signs or anything."

I let out the deep breath I had apparently been holding. "Okay, good. Thank you."

"No problem," she answered as she started to remove the

fetal monitor that was still attached to Addison's midsection. "Does he have a name yet?"

"Uhhhh," I began.

"Matthew Bennett," Addison said quietly. "It came to me today. I never got a chance to tell you. Matthew Bennett Hart, after your father and mine."

I leaned over and kissed her on the forehead. "It's perfect," I said, kissing her again. "Matthew Bennett it is."

An hour later, I walked into the neonatal intensive care unit where my boy had been taken. It was a large room with a couple dozen clear plastic boxes, each with a baby in it. They were tiny. So, so tiny. And they were all attached to a bunch of tubes.

A young, blond nurse approached me cautiously. "Can I help you?" she asked.

"Yeah, um, I got this wristband from the doctor," I said, holding up my wrist to show her. "They said my son was brought here when he was born a little while ago."

"Can I see your wristband, please?" I held it out for her, and she scanned it with some handheld device. It beeped once. "Oh, yes! Baby Boy Hart! Follow me and I'll take you to him."

"How's he doing, anyway?" I asked as I followed her. "They didn't tell us much when he was born."

"Considering how early he is, he's doing remarkably well," the nurse said. She rounded the corner to a smaller, more secluded area. There were only two incubators in this section, each with all the attached cords and monitors, and two rocking chairs.

I stopped walking as she approached the only incubator in use. "Is that him?" I asked, not quite sure what to do.

She smiled up at me. "Sure is. Come on over, Dad, and

meet your son. It won't hurt him to be close to him."

I walked slowly over to the box and finally looked inside. I could feel all the air whoosh out of my lungs like I'd been caught in an unexpected tackle.

He was smaller than I remembered from just a little while before. He had an IV in his tiny arm. An oxygen tube in his tiny nose. Little white circles attached to wires on his tiny chest. A little bandage with a glowing red light on his tiny toe.

And he was so damn beautiful. The most beautiful thing I had ever seen in my life, with the possible exception of my wife.

"According to his measurements, it looks like he is about fifteen inches long and weighs four pounds, five ounces," the nurse said. "He's a big boy!"

"That sounds really small to me."

"For a thirty-three weeker, that's actually very, very big," she responded. "If he had gone full term, he easily could have been over ten pounds."

I smiled, but I never took my eyes off my boy. I was so overwhelmed by what I was feeling. I was happy, so damn happy. And proud. And scared. And at peace.

"Would you like to hold him?" she asked me.

I whipped my head up to look at her. "I can hold him? Isn't he too sick for that?"

"I actually think he's strong enough to do what's called a Kangaroo Hold. It's skin-to-skin contact. We find that when the babies get to snuggle into their parents with nothing in the way, they recover faster," she explained. "They learn to regulate their temperatures better, eat better, grow faster. It's up to you, of course."

"Yeah!" I said with a smile. "I'd love to hold him. What do I do, just take off my shirt and sit down?"

"Let me go grab a couple of helpers, and we'll get you all set up," she answered. "Just hang tight for a minute and I'll be right back."

A couple minutes later she returned with a short, stout older nurse and a very tall, dark-headed woman. I don't think she was a nurse, but she was obviously staff of some sort.

"Okay, Mr. Hart, we're gonna have you take off your shirt and wrap your torso in this blanket, then sit down in this rocking chair," she started to explain. "We need to be able to get the baby to your bare chest, and then we'll wrap the blanket around you guys so you're wrapped in it together, okay?"

"Okay. But how am I going to hold him with all the wires?" I asked, feeling a little apprehensive. I didn't want to accidentally pull one of the tubes out of him or something.

"That's why there are two of us," she answered. "You just get ready to hold him and we'll worry about everything attached to him. Do you have a phone with you?"

"Yes, ma'am. I turned the volume off though."

"Go ahead and hand your phone to Mindy," she said, referring to the tall woman. "Make sure your camera is on, and once you two are settled, she'll take some pictures of the first time you hold your son."

"Really?" I asked, feeling the smile cross my face. "That would be . . . Yeah, thanks!" I handed her my phone and showed her the camera on it. It wasn't hard. I was sure she had used an iPhone before.

Once I got my shirt off and settled myself on the chair in the blanket, I watched as the two nurses opened the incubator and pulled my tiny little baby out. He squeaked as they organized all the cords, and they cooed at him as they worked.

"Are you ready?" the nurse asked one more time. I just nodded my head, feeling like I was about to burst.

The second his little baby skin touched me, I felt this weird feeling in my chest. I had never felt it before in my life. It's like my heart literally broke open from how much love I was experiencing. So this was what they meant when they said you loved your children so much it hurt.

The nurses worked quickly to show me where to put my hands and to wrap us up so he wouldn't get cold. I heard Mindy taking pictures, but it didn't really register. I was too busy looking at this tiny little bundle and feeling him in my hands. He was so small—he fit easily in one palm, which meant I could stroke his arms and his legs and his head with my other hand.

"We'll give you guys some privacy," the nurse said. "If you get uncomfortable or he starts to get really fussy, just say my name. I'm Kristen, and I'll be right around the corner."

"I'm Jason," I said, still not looking away from my son.

"Make sure to talk to him, Jason," Kristen said. "He recognizes your voice." With that, I was alone with my son for the very first time.

"Hey, little man," I said quietly as I looked down at his sweet face. I felt him snuggle into me, getting comfortable. He squeaked and grunted while he wiggled, making me laugh. "You're just a handsome boy, aren't you? You look just like your big brother, but with your mama's lips. I bet you have her smile, too, huh?"

I paused, just enjoying the feel of his little body up against mine while we rocked.

"I'm your daddy," I finally whispered. "And I'm so, so glad you're here. I've been dying to meet you ever since we found out you were coming. I know things are gonna be hard for the next couple of months with you being in the hospital and all, but I know you're a strong boy, Matty. You're strong like your mama. And strong like your brother. I'd say you were strong like me, but I'm pretty sure they kick my ass in the strength department these days." I chuckled. "I love you so much, little man. We're gonna get through this together, okay? I won't leave you to fight this on your own. I'll be here every step of the way."

I leaned my head down as much as I could and kissed him on the top of the head. I caught a whiff of his sweet baby scent, and I knew—*I knew*—I would never be the same man again.

I'd be better. Because I knew this little miracle was just the beginning of good things for this family.

Chapter Twenty-Three

It had been two months since Addison had seen Jaxon face-to-face. They were in the same hospital, but with her confined to one wing and him to another, she hadn't been allowed to see him. Sure, they had been FaceTiming whenever Jax was feeling up to it, but that wasn't every day. And the lighting was always low like he preferred. So Addison had never gotten a really good look at how bad off he was physically. Until now.

She gasped and her hands went over her mouth, tears filling her eyes. "Ohmygod," she half whispered. "Ohmygod, Jason, my baby boy. Ohmygod."

She walked over to Jaxon's bedside as fast as she could, given that she had given birth less than twenty-four hours before. As she got to his side, she collapsed on the chair next to him, and the tears started to flow.

"He . . ." she started. "He looks so, so sick, Jason. Ohmygod. How much weight has he lost?"

"About fifteen pounds."

She started stroking the soft peach-fuzz hair he had finally started to grow back. His lips were chapped, and there were deep, dark circles under his eyes. His skin coloring had a greyish sort of tint that was exaggerated by the low lighting he preferred.

"Does he sleep a lot?" she asked, eyes carefully looking over his entire body, as she started stroking his frail, skinny arms.

I sank down in the chair next to her, knowing I finally had to tell her everything. I had spent the last two months giving her information on a need-to-know basis to help keep her stress levels under control. But now that baby Matty had been born, there was no reason to hold anything back anymore. "He's been in a lot of pain lately, especially when it started spreading, so they've been giving him more pain meds. The meds tend to knock him out."

I heard her sniffle as she tried to take it all in. "So he's really dying," she said, her voice cracking. "I mean, I knew that the treatments weren't working, but to see him like this. Oh god, Jason. My baby is really dying."

I grabbed her hand but left her alone as she gently touched him as only a mother can. She was coming to grips with what I had known and kept from her for weeks.

This was really it.

We had one last chance. And it was a slim one.

We sat silently for what seemed like hours . . . me holding her hand. Her gently stroking Jaxon's hair, face, arms, hands. It was the worst moment of my life.

"Can you stay with him a second?" she asked as she stood up and wiped her eyes. "I need to use the restroom really fast. Post-birth issues and all."

I smiled weakly at her as she made her way to the other

room.

"Daddy?" I heard Jaxon say weakly. He had only called me that once before, right after we had been talking about his late father, Austin, and he was falling asleep. I wasn't positive if he was asking for me or Austin. "Daddy?" he said again.

"Hey," I said gently, leaning over the bed and stroking his head. "Are you looking for me, buddy? I'm right here."

"I had a dream about you," he said, so quietly I almost couldn't hear him. "I dreamed that we were playing football together." I smiled. "We were both on the Cowboys, Daddy. And we kept tackling the other quarterback together."

I chuckled. "Who was it? I know a few we could take down."

He adjusted himself on his bed and licked his lips, eyes still closed. "I don't know. But he wasn't very good. And we were the best."

"That's cause we *are* the best, buddy," I said, moving his pillow to help get him more comfortable. "We're a great team."

"Jason?" he asked.

"What do you need?" I picked up his tiny, fragile hand.

"I don't wanna call you Jason anymore," he said. "You're my dad. Can I call you that, now?"

I wasn't expecting my heart to swell with emotion like it did. But sure enough, after trying to hold it together for my family for so long, tears started sliding down my cheeks. "I would be so honored if you called me that, Jax," I whispered, trying not to lose control of my emotions, and making him smile as he settled into his bed again. "Nothing would make me happier." I kissed him on the head as he started to fall asleep.

"Can we go to camp with Bri this summer, Daddy?" he

asked as he finally gave in to sleep.

I chuckled. "We'll see, buddy," I said as I tucked the blanket in around him. "I hope so."

I heard a sniffle behind me and turned to see Addison shuffling back over. She had tears running down her face too.

"I take it you heard all that?" I asked, still wanting to drink in the moment.

She sat down and started touching Jax again. "You know how they say moms have several moments with their kids that they will always hide in their hearts and never forget?" I nodded. My mother used to tell me that every once in a while. "That was definitely one of those moments."

We sat quietly again for a while, lost in our own thoughts, watching Jaxon sleep. His time was running out and we both knew it. Because there was nothing we could do, we were just content to sit quietly together.

A while later, there was a soft knock on the door. We turned to see Kristina stick her head in.

"Hey," she said quietly. "Do you guys have a second to come chat out here with me?"

I took a deep breath and stood up, bringing Addison with me.

As we stepped into the hall, we knew that any news Kristina brought us could be really good, or really bad. At this point, it could go either way. I put my arms around Addison as she wrapped hers around my waist. We were clinging to each other, bracing ourselves for the worst.

"I'm going to get right to the point and not drag it out," Kristina said. "The results of the test came in. The cord blood isn't a one hundred percent match." I held my breath. "But it's close enough that we can use it and probably will be able to do so successfully."

My eyes closed, and I felt myself breathe out. Addison stayed quiet. "So we can use it . . . but are we *allowed* to? Legally."

"I just got the call." Kristina smiled. "It's been approved by both the CDC and the IRB, so it's time to get those signatures from you now."

I felt myself begin to cry, feeling Addison shaking as she did the same.

"It will take us a few days to set everything up," she continued. "But we'll do the transplant within the week. Congrats, guys. We did it."

Burying my face in Addison's neck, I couldn't contain the sobs that came out of me. Jaxon, my son, finally got a match. His baby brother—the surprise baby we weren't trying for, the baby Addison worked so hard to carry to term—was probably going to save his big brother's life.

That tiny spark of hope I had when this had all started so many months before was back. And it wasn't so tiny anymore.

Chapter TWENTY-FOUR

Less than a week later, the transplant went off without much of a hitch. It took a couple days for Dr. Bates to be sure the cord blood was doing what it was supposed to do, and that Jaxon's body was responding well to it. It would take months for Jaxon to be back to normal. He had lots of weight to put back on and some hair to grow, but within a few days, he didn't need as many pain meds and his skin started to return to a more normal color.

Even ten days later, I still wasn't allowed to see him very often, because being a post-transplant patient, he was basically in isolation. And even then, I had to beg Dr. Bates to make an exception. Anytime I entered the room, I had to be thoroughly scrubbed down and dressed in sterile clothing, always, always wearing a mask over my face and gloves on my hands. Any sniffle or sneeze meant I was denied for a full twenty-four hours. It was brutal but necessary.

"Hey bud," I said as I walked in the door of the hospital room he had been in for so long. "Whatcha doing?"

"Playing Minecraft," he said, not taking his eyes off the TV.

"How're you feeling?"

"Um, I'm kind of hungry, actually." Still no eye contact.

"Really? That's a good sign. What do you want to eat?"

He was quiet for a minute, probably distracted from food by the creeper who was stealing all his tools, or something like that. Finally, he paused the game.

"I want a really large cheese pizza," he said, eyes wide as he described it. "I want to have lots and lots of cheese on top. And I want it to have cheese in the crust, like that kind we saw on TV. Can we have that, Daddy? Please?"

I smiled at him. I would never get tired of hearing him call me that. Ever.

"I'm not sure Dr. Bates will approve of delivery quite yet. But tell ya what," I answered. "Why don't I see what kind of Jell-O crap they make you eat today and then we can Facetime Deuce and watch him eat the biggest pizza like that that he can find. We'll have some men time. Maybe we can even patch in your Pee-paw."

"Oh yeah. I guess Deuce doesn't have that much practice anymore since they didn't make the playoffs," he said somberly, obviously not happy over the pizza. He could have pitched a fit about it, but he was a real trooper about it all.

I chuckled. "Just don't remind Deuce about that. He's still pretty upset by that loss to the Ravens. We wouldn't want to make him cry."

"Deuce cries?" Jaxon asked, eyes wide.

"Only every year when he doesn't get that Super Bowl ring," I said, standing up and clapping my hands together. "So, we'll put in that call, but in the meantime, I have a surprise for you."

"You do?"

"Yep. Feel like taking this wheelchair for a spin?"

"Sure," he said. "Can I put on some shorts first? I'm tired of so many people seeing my butt."

I snorted. "Sure, buddy. We can't have that."

I helped Jaxon into the bathroom, where he could do his business and put on some shorts in privacy. Once I got him set up, I made a quick call to Deuce while I waited for Jax to get ready. He was still really weak, so it took a while. But one thing about Jaxon . . . he was determined to get back to normal. Even if that meant some very slow practice on everyday things like using the bathroom.

"Dad!" he called out. "I'm ready. Can you help me?"

I rolled the wheelchair up to the bathroom door and helped him shuffle over to it. Once he was settled, we got him all geared up as well. We'd gotten special clearance to leave the room since we were headed straight to another sterile environment, but I didn't want to pick up any unnecessary germs on the way.

"Where are you two headed?" Bri called as we wheeled past her station.

"Just going on a little road trip," I called back.

I heard her laugh as we made our way around the corner. "Have fun!"

"Where are we really going?" Jaxon asked as we made our way inside the elevators.

"It's a surprise, buddy!"

"It better include that cheese pizza," he said, making me chuckle.

Once we reached the fifth floor, I pushed him down the hall and stopped in front of the door.

"Here, bud," I said, reaching for his wrist. "I need you to

put it on."

"What is it?" he asked as I put the plastic bracelet around his wrist.

"You'll see."

As I pushed open the door, Kristen looked up. "Hey there, Jason! I see you brought company." She walked over and scanned our wrists like normal.

"Kristen, this is my son, Jaxon. Matty's big brother."

"It's very nice to meet you," she said with a smile. "Would you like to meet your little brother?"

"I can see him now?" Jaxon asked with a huge grin, peeking out from behind his mask. "We're here to see the baby?"

"Yep," I answered. "Dr. Bates said we can't stay long, so you don't overdo it. But he said it's okay for us to come up for a short visit since it has to be super clean in here, too."

"Yeah!" Jaxon half yelled, half whispered. It was clear he realized where he was and didn't want to disturb any of the babies.

As we strolled through the NICU and headed to our little corner, Jaxon looked around, wide-eyed at all the incubators. "Do all of those things have babies in them?" he asked.

"Most of them," Kristen answered. "When a baby is born too early, they have a hard time staying warm. So we keep them in the incubator to keep them nice and toasty."

As we rounded the corner, we saw Addison sitting in the rocking chair, wrapped up in a kangaroo hold. When she opened her eyes and saw us, her face lit up with the biggest, brightest smile I had seen on her face in a while.

"Hey guys," she said as she rocked. "Are you here to see the latest addition to our family? Kristen, can you hand me a face mask?"

I wheeled Jax up right next to Addison so he could see

Matty up close and personal as Kristen helped Addison get the mask on.

"Wow," he breathed. "Is that him?"

"It is," Addison said. "Jaxon, meet your new baby brother, Matthew. Matty, this is your big brother, Jaxon."

"Hi Matty," Jaxon said, his entire focus on his new brother. "Can I touch him?"

"Sure," Addison said, shifting the blanket a bit. "Since he still has all these wires stuck to him, why don't you start stroking his hand and his arm. He likes that."

As Jaxon reached over to touch the baby, Matty opened his eyes and looked right at Jax. As if he knew this was his brother, Matty grabbed onto Jaxon's finger just as he started stroking his little fingers.

"He's so tiny, Mom," Jaxon said, looking at up at her with concern in his eyes. "Is he gonna be okay?"

"He's gonna be just fine," Addison said as I pulled out my phone and started taking some candid snapshots. "When babies are born this little, they just need a little extra help finishing their development. So he needs to grow a little bit more in the hospital like he should have done in my belly."

As I listened to Addison explain what every single wire and tube did, I couldn't help the overwhelming feeling of joy I was having. Yes, these were private moments between us, but I wanted so bad to send them to Adam and have him post them everywhere. I was so proud of these three. Jaxon for hanging on until we could find a treatment. Addison for pushing through until Matty was ready to be born. Matty for coming to us at the exact right time to save his brother's life. I was so full of pride I almost wanted to burst.

My family had made it through a terrible time. Arguably the hardest time we would ever have in our lives. But not only did we do it, we came out stronger. And a bigger family unit.

Deuce could have that ring if he wanted. No Super Bowl win would ever compare to this.

Chapter TWENTY-FIVE

I walked through the tunnel at Mile High Stadium. Immediately upon stepping on the field, I heard the crowds roar. I looked around, absorbing the fans decked out in their favorite jerseys, waving foam fingers in the air.

So this is what the Super Bowl looked like from the field. It was like a dream come true.

Except it wasn't my Super Bowl.

Jaxon and Matty were both still in the hospital, but they were doing well. And Addison and I had agreed that this appearance was too important for me to miss.

As I made my way over to the fifty-yard line, dressed in my street clothes, I heard the announcement begin.

My name is Jason Hart. You may know me as the defensive lineman for the Dallas Cowboys, but you may not recognize me playing the more important role in my life . . . the role of Dad.

I looked up at the Jumbotron to see various pictures of me and the boys scroll by. There were shots of Jaxon decked out in his Cowboy gear. One from that Halloween a couple years ago when he was a football player and I was a banana. A good-looking candid from the wedding when we both wore tuxedos. And several of him in the hospital.

As you probably know, my nine-year-old son, Jaxon, was diagnosed with Acute Lymphoblastic Leukemia, or ALL, last summer. While ALL has a ninety percent cure rate, Jaxon was one of those who had to fight a little harder than most.

My eyes welled up a bit as the montage of Jaxon in the hospital started. He was still there. It had only been a couple of weeks since the transplant. But he was improving so quickly that seeing pictures of him so sick was surreal.

When our attempts to find a bone marrow donor for Jaxon within our family failed, we began looking at outside resources like bone marrow donation registries. What we discovered was a severe lack of donors to meet the growing demands of those with childhood cancer. That's when the idea for Hart to Heart was born.

Our goal is to bring awareness of this need to the forefront of the public and to encourage people to join the bone marrow registry. Won't you please join us on this very important quest?

Our miracle finally happened with the birth of our second son, Baby Matthew. You can be the miracle for another child in need. You can save a life. Please consider joining us by checking out our website, harttoheart.net.

I got to the fifty-yard line and smiled as I saw Roger and Joy join me.

"Hey, man," I said, shaking his hand and clapping his shoulder. "How's it going?"

"It's great," he said as I hugged Joy. "Thanks for doing this for us. We haven't had a vacation together in years, so this is really nice. Thank you."

"No problem," I said as I was handed a microphone by one of the stadium staff members. "This wouldn't be happening if it weren't for you."

"What do you mean?" he asked.

I smiled as I heard the announcement start. *Ladies and Gentleman, please welcome Jason Hart, who is joined by Roger and Joy Chilla.*

As we waited for the cheers to die down a bit, Roger looked at me like he couldn't figure out what I was up to. He knew part of why they were here. I wasn't going to start spouting off personal information in front of millions of spectators around the world without their permission. But they didn't know everything.

"Roger, Joy, we met under the worst circumstances people can ever meet . . . while fighting for the lives of our children," I began consciously trying to not lower the microphone while I was speaking into it. "But a particular conversation we had in the hallway of the children's oncology ward at Texas Memorial Children's Hospital really stuck with me. It changed the way I look at certain issues." The stadium attendant handed me a shiny, wooden plaque. It had a new logo and a picture of their baby girl, Iris, smiling wide for the camera.

"I am proud to present this plaque to you as a way to honor the newest department in the Hart to Heart organization, called Iris's Umbrella."

I handed it to Joy and watched as Roger put his arms around her when she wiped away the tears that had already started falling.

"It is because of Iris that this particular issue was brought to light. As you informed me, so many families are stuck between making too much money to qualify for any assistance on medical bills, and insurance that has already been capped and won't pay for any more treatments. We hope we can honor Iris's memory by providing some much-needed assistance to those families."

"Thank you," Roger mouthed through his tears.

"Don't thank me yet," I said. "There's more."

Roger and Joy both looked up at me in surprise. What they didn't know is that in its short life, Hart to Heart had raised more than just awareness to the issues of bone marrow donation. It had drawn in millions of dollars in donations. So much so that Adam had already hired a director and a financial officer. In total, Hart to Heart already had six paid staff members because it was growing so rapidly.

"As the ones who sparked the idea for the Iris's Umbrella division, we thought it was only fitting that you guys also be the very first recipients of its assistance." I paused to hand them an oversized check, made out to them. "Our treasury department has been in contact with the hospital, and as of this morning, all of Iris's outstanding medical bills have now been paid."

As the crowd roared, Roger's and Joy's eyes went wide, and their mouths dropped open.

"Are you serious?" Roger asked.

"It's all covered," I said, handing the mic back to the attendant so we could talk more privately. "Hospital, doctors, surgeries, everything. You guys are in the clear now."

"I . . . just . . ." He finally gave up what he was trying to say and came in for a hug, Joy following closely behind him until the three of us were in a bear hug together, the two of them crying and me trying not to start boohooing too.

It was one of those moments that I knew would be imprinted on my brain forever. And I realized if this was the only time I ever stepped on the field during the Super Bowl, it was worth it.

EPILOGUE

JULY

"I can't believe you talked me into this," Deuce complained as we walked across the grass towards the pavilion. "I have sweat in my butt crack. Do you know how much I hate butt sweat?"

I chuckled. "Don't even try to convince me that you aren't having a good time. It's the best time of the year, man! It says so in the camp song we sing every morning!"

He grumbled as we kept walking towards our dinner. It was our fifth night at Camp HopesALot, the pediatric oncology camp Jaxon had wanted so badly to attend.

As soon as Jax was released to go home after his transplant, I'd put in a call to Bri, who made sure we were contacted when it was time to register. She also let me know how badly they needed volunteers, especially male volunteers. So Deuce and I signed up.

We all agreed it wouldn't be the best thing for us to be

camp counselors. Especially Deuce. No telling what kind of chaos would occur if he had access to twenty little boys who were liable to follow him into whatever prank he could come up with.

Instead, we were running a football clinic out on the big field to the west of the camp. July in Texas is brutally hot; everyone knows that. But July, near Dallas, when you are standing out in a field all day long, chasing around a bunch of rowdy campers with virtually no shade . . . Well, let's just say that neither of us would ever complain about the heat at training camp again.

When we got to the pavilion, where we were all going to enjoy some catered barbecue for dinner, we bypassed the line and made our way over to the ladies. It was talent show night, so several guests were able to visit. Addison and Vanessa were invited.

I saw baby Matty before I saw Addison. Even at six months old, he looked so much like Jaxon it was amazing. The only real difference was his hair. It was the same shade of brown as Addison's. Jaxon's, however, had changed.

Once his chemo was finished and his hair started coming back in, it was dark. Very dark, like mine. Addison and I joked that it just made our family more color coordinated. Jax took after me and Matty took after her.

I jogged up to the two of them as Deuce took off for Vanessa and Trace. I swooped Matty into my arms, tossing him into the air.

"Hey, little man," I said, giving him kisses all over his chubby cheeks as he squealed and grabbed at my ears. "I miss you, buddy. Are you ready for daddy to come home?" He patted my cheeks and smiled the bright grin he had so obviously gotten from his mama.

"I think we're all ready for daddy to come home," Addison said, putting her arms around my waist.

"Mmmm," I growled in her ear. "Don't say things like that, woman, or I might have to skip the clinics tomorrow and show up at that fancy bed and breakfast you're staying in so I can introduce you to some of my better tackling moves." I kissed her forehead as she giggled.

She knew I wasn't kidding, though. Once Matty was born, the countdown was on for me. I had anxiously awaited that six-week appointment clearing Addison for "activities." The day the doctor gave us the all-clear, I drove straight to Deuce's house, handed Matty over to Vanessa, and took Addison home, where I had my way with her until it was time for her to nurse again.

I had spent most of my life thinking sex was just sex. But my mother had been right all along . . . there was something special about that connection with your spouse. I couldn't describe it. I couldn't explain it. And I wasn't going to try. But I did make it a point to connect with her every single day until we left for camp. I even convinced her to lock the bedroom door at night so we could get busy. It was a wonder we hadn't gotten pregnant again, yet.

Needless to say, I never had to explain wall sex to Jaxon. And the wall got quite a workout several times. There were advantages to being my size and having to work out every day for my job.

Just then, I saw Jaxon making his way over to us. He still wasn't one hundred percent back to normal. He got winded easily and took naps during the day. He spent a good chunk of his day at camp being pushed in a wheelchair as they made their way to activities. But every day he was gaining strength. Enough so that he was looking forward to starting back at school. Apparently a year of tutoring was long enough, even for someone like Jax.

"Mom! Matty!" he yelled as he reached for his brother, immediately making funny faces to make him laugh. The two of them were practically inseparable at home. Being nine and a half years apart, we never expected them to be so close. But the age difference had some advantages. Jax never got jealous of the baby, and Matty always had someone to dote on him.

I was a little worried about when they got older, though. No telling what kinds of trouble they would get into together at some point.

"Are you having fun at camp, Jax?" Addison asked. She had resigned herself months ago to the fact that when it came between her and Matty, Jaxon went to Matty first. Every single time.

"It's so fun, Mom!" he said, using his hands to emphasize everything he said. "I learned how to shoot a bow and arrow today! And then went in a canoe! And the other day I rode a real horse, Mom. A real horse! It was huge!"

"Sounds like it was worth being away from home for the week."

"Oh yeah! We even get to have a big ol' food fight tomorrow! Where we throw Jell-O and whipped cream at all our friends and our counselors. Can you believe that? I can't wait to come back next year! Will you come back, too, Dad? Will you? Please?"

I ruffled his hair as I handed Matty back to Addison. "I'd love to," I said. "I'll have to check on training camp first, ya know."

This year, it had worked out that camp ended five days before we had to report to California. So we decided to make a family vacation out of it. Addison and Vanessa were staying at a swanky B&B a few miles away for the week while Deuce, Jaxon, and I stayed in cabins at camp. Once Saturday rolled around, we would head back to Dallas and spend a couple days taking the boys to Six Flags and the Dallas Zoo.

It was a short family vacation, and we were staying in our own house, but after a week of camp and Jaxon still recuperating, we needed to be close to home. Plus, Addison and I agreed that Camp HopesALot was important. Not just for Jaxon, but for us, too. We'd been where all these kids' parents had been. Our priorities and our outlook were completely changed. As long as we could support it in some way, we would.

When she sat down at the picnic table to finish eating, I kissed the top of her head again. "I'll be right back. I'm going to get my plate."

She nodded at me, then shifted her attention back to the boys who were playing peek-a-boo, Matty on her lap and Jaxon standing next to them.

As I got in line, I couldn't take my eyes off my little family. We had been through the ringer over the past year, and we made it through together.

I was in awe of them and how much strength they had. And they didn't even realize it.

Addison cared for both of them without thinking twice and pushed through a hard pregnancy to give them both the best chance of survival possible.

Jaxon caused us to be in the right place at the right time, saving his brother from a severely premature birth.

And Matty surprised us by coming into our lives at a point when most people wouldn't want to have another baby. And bringing with him the one thing we needed to save Jaxon from a terminal illness.

They weren't perfect. But they were *mine*.

They were my superheroes.
And they would forever be my Hart.

The End

AUTHOR'S NOTE

For eight years, I was a volunteer at a camp similar to Camp HopesALot. These camps are real places doing real work for real children with very real cancer. They are wonderful camps where children who have had any kind of cancer can convene with other children who have been there and who "get it." Some even allow a sibling to attend as well.

During my time at camp, I was privy to overhearing discussions about the changes in their hair after chemo, to kids learning to feel comfortable walking outside without a hat on to hide their bald head, to grieving their lost friends in a safe environment.

I have seen some of these kids grow up, get married, and live successful, happy lives. I have also seen some of these kids never make it to adulthood.

The experiences and friendships I made during my eight years left a mark on me that has changed the way I feel about childhood cancers.

One of these wonderful camps is Camp iHope. Camp iHope is completely self-funded and relies on donations to stay up and running every summer. If you are so moved, please consider making a donation to them. You can get more information at http://www.campihope.org/donate.html.

Also, the need for potential bone marrow donors is great. If you have never considered joining the registry, please, please consider doing so. It is free to be a donor—all medical costs will be covered at no cost to you—and you can change your mind at any time. Although I hope you don't.

Donors between the ages of 18 and 44, and especially donors of mixed race, are highly sought out. There is no guarantee you will ever be called to donate (I've been on the registry for over fifteen years and have yet to match anyone), but each additional potential donor increases the chances for the recipient in need.

For more information, check out http://bethematch.org.

ACKNOWLEDGMENTS

This was a very, very difficult book for me to write. Not just technically, but emotionally as well. So there are quite a few people I need to thank along the way.

KRISTIN SHELDON . . . I cannot thank you enough for sitting down with me that January afternoon at Starbucks, hearing the storyline I had running through my head, and giving me every piece of information I needed to make the medical parts work with the story parts. You were VITALLY important to getting this endeavor off the ground. Of course, then you threw your cute baby at me, smothered me in her baby pheromones and promptly got me pregnant. But whatever. I can overlook that part since you helped me so much . . . :)

TIFFANY PLUNKETT-YANCICH . . . Some of my best memories are of watching campers chase after wheelchairs, goats trying to bite my fingers off, and dressing up like fools . . . all for the sake of a good time. I cherish those memories with you, friend! Thank you for reading over a book you may never have picked up otherwise and making sure all the medical stuff jived with reality. And especially for understanding why this book was so very, very important to me. Keep doing the good work you are doing and you know I support you guys 100%!

BRIANNE AND KRISTINA . . . From campers to counselors. From children to adults. From campers to friends. It has been my pleasure to watch you two beat childhood cancer and grow into beautiful, married women with careers. I'm so very, very proud of you both in more ways than you will ever understand. Brianne, I will always think of you as my mini-me, whether you like it or not. I'm old, so I'm allowed. And Kristina . . . you kicked cancer's ass once. You can do it again. I believe in you and am praying you through!

KAREN LAWSON . . . I can never thank you enough for sharing your heart and your experiences about the time your own child went through chemo. Your insight into the emotional side was possibly the most important piece of this puzzle. I told you before I started, if I couldn't do this story justice, I would never publish it. You helped me make it as realistic as possible. So thank you! Love you, friend!

MEGAN KAPUSTA . . . You are always the first to read for me and always the first to get back to me. You see things I don't and have a knack for making sure my timelines are always spot on! Your eye just amazes me sometimes. And your reliability always calms me down when I start stressing about getting things done. You are INVALUABLE to me! I cannot thank you enough!

DAWN L. CHILETZ . . . I honestly don't know how we get it all done. Reading, writing, beta reading, editing, formatting, publishing, marketing . . . the list is endless. Thank you for your valuable feedback and the endless stream of PM's. Even when I disappear in the middle of the conversations because something comes up. Just knowing you are behind me is huge for me.

SARA NEY . . . Yes, you are a pain in my ass. But mostly, I just adore your face. Sometimes, all I need is for you to drop an f-bomb at me and tell me something stupid to get me back on track. And you understand that more than anyone else. Plus, you jumped up and helped me out SO MUCH when I was stressing. I cannot thank you enough for that. Now stop blaming me for your accidental porn subscription. That was all your own fault.

AE WOODWARD . . . Just . . . thank you. Your words give me confidence and make me feel like I can do this. So . . . thank you.

THE "REAL" LINDSAY . . . Hey, you didn't totally suck as a beta reader this time! I'll turn you into a real book nerd yet!

MURPHY RAE . . . I don't really know what to say that hasn't already been said. You rock as an editor. You rock as a cover designer. You rock as a friend. You just rock. And I can't imagine ever going through an endeavor like this without you.

JULIE TITUS . . . Beyond your ability to format books, thank you for just being you. Your demeanor is so very calming when I can't remember dates or timelines. Thank you for answer the same questions over and over and over for me because my brain kept falling apart.

KRISTIN DELCAMBRE AND MEGAN GUNTER . . . My final line of defense. You two are freaking amazing. A-MAZ-ING! Thank you for your critical eye and seeing things others miss. It's always a good sign when your formatter says, "This is one of the cleanest books I've formatted in years."

BRENDA ROTHERT, KATHRYN PEREZ, COLLEEN HOOVER . . . My writing mentors. My writing friends. Just thank you for supporting me through this book and through this pregnancy. None of it has been easy so thank you for all the grace you have given me and the friendship you have offered.

BABY BUG . . . Dude. You threw this project off track by making me so sick for so long. But buddy, the hormones came at the right time. I was able to feel and express things I wouldn't have been able to otherwise. And as bitchy as I am about it, I really am looking forward to meeting you and snuggling you and finding out if you are, in fact, a ninja or just like pretending to be multiple times a day. Remind me never to give you sugar. You're already hyper.

MY KIDS AND HUSBAND . . . With the first book, you threw me a bone so I could try something new. With this one, you supported me 100% and encouraged me and helped me. I know I spend hours on the computer. I know it's frustrating. But know this . . . it is all for you guys. Everything I do is for you guys. We're not a perfect family. But we're MINE. And that's the most important thing to me.

THE "REAL" DR. DON BATES . . . You will probably never read this book. You will probably never know a character is based on you. But you were my very first experience with childhood cancer. I watched you, as an elementary schooler, fight your battle with leukemia. I watched you win. I watched you grow to become one of the best pediatric oncologists in the country. Me and my family prayed relentlessly for your health when I was a child. While I didn't completely understand what was happening, the experience changed me. Your character is based on you to honor you and your desire to take your experiences and use them to help other children. To that, I say, "Well done." I hope to never have to be in a situation like this. But if I do . . . I am coming to you first.

FINALLY . . . THE CAMP KIDS AND PARENTS . . . You all inspired this story. I can never adequately express how much you all mean to me. It would be impossible for you to understand how your strength and fight changed me to my core. Thank you. This story is in honor of you.

ABOUT THE AUTHOR

M.E. Carter didn't set out to write a book. She just had a random story rolling around in her head after working with her local PTA. Then one day, it became all-consuming and had to be written down. This should come as no big surprise since she has always had random stories rolling around in her head and even wrote an episode of CHiPS at age 11. (She was the guest star, of course.)

She lives in Texas with her husband and three children, Mary, Elizabeth and Carter. Get it? ;)

You can follow her on Facebook at:
https://www.facebook.com/authorMECarter

on Twitter at
https://twitter.com/AuthorMECarter

or email her at
AuthorMECarter@gmail.com

Made in the USA
San Bernardino, CA
28 September 2016